The Female Don Dada

Part 2

Kateri & Yara Kaleemah

Copyright © 2017

DEDICATION

We want to Thank both of our supporters. We thank you for always being there for us. We hope that you enjoy this story and please let us know if we should work together in the future.

Enjoy!!!!

Karma Strikes

Marquis had turned her life upside down. After finding out that he was her worst enemy, Grace had to recount all her steps. She had been too trusting, allowing people into her life when she had no clue who they were. She had tried to tell Pop that she wasn't made for this game. She was too soft and didn't have her father's ruthless attitude and iron fist. But he wouldn't listen. She was still a little girl when he died. But he trusted her and it was her job to carry out his and Jr.'s legacy. It seemed like she had failed.

The man she loved had betrayed her so when she looked at her son she felt nothing but sorrow. She killed his father without an ounce of remorse. She would one day have to explain to him that there weren't any friends in this game. The same people that sat at the table and broke bread with you could be the same people to hunt you down and kill you. Murda had a whole team of low life snakes, she just couldn't believe that Marquis was one of them.

"What the fuck?" Grace looked in the rear-view mirror as the police motioned for her to pull over.

"Stay calm," Bev told her.

"What the fuck is going on?" Grace asked nervously.

The officer approached the car, drawing his gun. Her heart was drumming in her chest. She knew that the day would come but she was praying that it wouldn't be so soon. She closed her eyes and then, looked back at her son.

"Mommy loves you, my sweet baby boy."

He smiled at her with warm eyes, "I love you too Momma."

The officer tapped on the window. "Grace Lee? This car has been reported stolen, ma'am."

"What?"

3

"Put your hands on the steering wheel and don't move," he told her, raising the gun.

Grace bit her bottom lip. "Officer, my son is in the backseat," she explained. "Can we do this nicely?"

"Ma'am, step out of the car." he opened the door, "and put your hands on the hood." He pulled her out of the car and started to pat her down. "Grace Lee, you are under arrest for the murder of Marquis Anderson. Anything you say can and will…"

"What?" Bev hopped out of the car. "What's happening? Where are you taking her?" she asked.

"Ma'am, get back in the car," he said as he pointed his gun at her.

Grace cried, "Please, Bev, just get in the car. Take him home."

Bev watched as he cuffed Grace and then put her into the back seat of the squad car. After a few minutes, she collected herself and climbed into the driver's seat. With all the recent police killings, it could have been much worse. She took a deep breath and assured Jr. that everything would be okay. The police cruiser sped off and she went in the opposite direction. She had to call a lawyer for Grace.

A New Queen Emerges

~Bev~

Mother fuckers got the game all the way fucked up if they think I am about to run this shit the way that Drama had. She was so naïve to think that any of these people had her best interest at heart anyway. Hell, I don't even know why she trusted me. I guess it made things easier to find out that I am her sister but now that Murda was out of the way it was time for me to deviate back to my father's ways. This empire Drama was trying to build is going to be put back in order. For starters, I am firing everybody who thought they worked for her. New money, new business.

I would be the first to say that I support Fuzz in wanting to pursue a law career so his ass going to have to go to work, too. I hired him to help Drama get out of her case. I knew them worm ass cops didn't have anything on her. So, if she knows like I know she better not say a damn thing to prove otherwise.

Picking up the phone I pulled up the real estate site and started scrolling through the commercial properties near our old bathroom. I found a small office building on Boston Post Road and called the listing agent.

"Hello, I am looking at the office building on Boston Post Rd. I am interested in coming to see it. Is there someone I can talk to about it?" I asked.

"Hello, hold on one minute and I will get Brandi for you. What is your name?" She asked.

"Oh, I am so sorry. My name is Beverly." I answered.

"Thank you, Ms. Beverly, let me get Brandi the listing agent for you."

"Thank you." I said.

"Hello. Ms. Beverly! This is Brandi. I understand that you are interested in the property on Boston Post Road. What can I tell you about it?' She asked.

"I want to know everything about it. I would like to schedule an appointment to come and see it." I answered.

"Well are you free right now? We can look at it now."

"Yes, I am I can meet you in about an hour. I'll be driving a silver Mercedes."

"Great! The door will be open, just come on in!"

"I will see you then!" I said hanging up with her.

Then, my line beeped with a collect call from Drama. I accepted the call and pressed the phone to my ear. My sister sounded so pitiful but for now, she had to take one for the team.

"Hey girl, what are y'all doing?" She asked nonchalantly.

"Hey. I ain't doing a damn thing but waiting on this pizza." I told her.

"Don't get too fat over there." There was a brief silence on the phone.

Grace was trying to act as if prison life wasn't eating her ass up. She probably cried every time she took a shower. There wasn't any cinnamon body wash and candles behind the wall. I tried to cheer her up by talking about the kids and my unborn baby.

"Tracey said he was coming to see you today. You know he doesn't discuss much about the case with me. I have to find out through the grapevine." I sucked my teeth. "But I hope you get out soon cuz I'ma need you to help me with your niece when she gets here."

"And who told you it was a girl?" Drama laughed. "That's Fuzz's big-headed ass boy in there. Let us pray that he don't be nothing like his daddy, though."

"Shut up! It's my little princess in there." I rubbed my stomach.

"Your call has two minutes left." The operator interrupted.

"Well, kiss my baby for me, sis." Drama sighed on the phone.

I sighed too, "You know I will sis. I love you."

"Love you more." She hung up.

I waddled my fat pregnant ass downstairs to open the door for the pizza delivery guy. Then, went into the kitchen to eat it before I had to go meet with the realtor. I arrived at the office and met with Brandi. She walked me around as I asked questions about the building.

"What is the neighborhood like?" I asked.

"It is mostly comprised of doctors, dentist. There are a few stores spread around. Such as a pharmacy and a small bakery. Behind us is a residential area where most of the business owners live. Not too much traffic around here.

"Great I need for my workers to stay focused."

"Well here they will be. This building boasts three floors with a finished basement with 4 small offices. On each floor, there is two bathrooms and six offices. As you saw when you came in, you have a large reception area. All the windows are one way. You can see out, but people can't see in. This building was built in 2003 and is beautiful sculptured."

"This sounds perfect. How much is it to purchase the whole building?" I asked.

"Well, to lease will be $25,000, and to purchase will be $500,000.00." She answered.

"Well let me talk to my banker and see what I can do. This is a perfect place for my export business."

"Oh yeah, what are you exporting?" She asked.

"Toys for needy children. I already have a small operation, But I need to expand with our economy." I answered.

"That is such a true statement. Well if you need any help, I can also put you in touch with some people that can help." She stated.

"Thank you so much for the offer, but I have been working with some of the best staff for years, and they know what I want and have been with me for years. Again, thank you though."

"Well my offer stands at any time." She said shaking my hand.

"It was a pleasure speaking with you. I will be in touch with you tomorrow, after I speak to my banker." I said returning her hand shake.

"Great, looking forward to it!" She said getting in her car.

I got in my car and looked around the neighborhood. I had to be careful about the nosey housewives around here. They can be so nosey, and I don't need them to start nosing around. I would use the Basement to cook up the drugs and the first and second floors to pack them, the third would be our offices. Fuzz could even use one of the offices.

I have been working on a new synthetic drug and I think this would be a wonderful place to mass produce it. With very few fumes, I should be safe. Picking up the phone, I decided to call my banker and lease the building for a few months and then purchase it. I didn't want to draw attention from the IRS. Our businesses were doing good, but any step up is always noticed. He agreed with me and said that he would have a check for three months' rent messengered over to Brandi in the morning. I needed to go home and think out the plan.

When I arrived, Mama had already cooked dinner and everyone was waiting on me to get back. We sat down and said grace, talked and ate. I decided to take a break for the rest of the evening. The baby was kicking up a storm and I was tired. First thing in the morning, I would meet with Fuzz and the boys and go over everything with them. I was excited about seeing my husband. I haven't seen him in over a week. Sitting in bed, I sketched out the layout for the building and drifted off to sleep.

I awoke to a gentle kiss on my forehead.

"Wake up babe!" Fuzz whispered.

"Morning babe, when did you get here?" I asked.

"I just got here a few minutes ago, G is downstairs cooking. Look at you! My boy is getting big in there." He laughed.

"Oh hush, I'm getting big because of you. And it's my girl. There are no boys in here!" I laughed.

"We will see what is in there in a month. But I already know what's in there. Now what is this drawing about." He said picking up the notebook.

"I just closed on a building that I want to work out of. Those are the plans of how I want the layout done. So, I need to have people come in and start the work. I was also hoping that you could work out of there, so we could be closer to each other."

"I like these plans. And I see that you wasted no time taking the game to the next level. Do you have the keys? I can go by and have the guys start working now. Were you planning on putting the scientist for your new drug in there also?"

"Yes, I want to build a lab for them in the basement, the first floor will be where they pack and ship the product."

"Sounds like a good idea. High end building for high end clients! My baby is pretty and has brains!"

"Yes, she does, and my husband is handsome and strong."

"Well get up, I'm starving, and you know how G is about meal time."

"Yeah I know. Let me get up."

Just then I heard a pop and I felt like I was using the bathroom on myself. Then suddenly, a sharp pain raced across my abdomen forcing me to bend over in pain.

"Hmm babe? Look!"

"Oh, my God, is that your water breaking."

"Naw, Sherlock, I peed on myself! Yes, my water broke. Go get G!" I screamed.

"G her water broke!" Fuzz said yelling!

"What do you mean, she is early! Call the ambulance!"

I knew those two would panic so I called the ambulance. Went to get dressed and grabbed my bag. By the time I got downstairs, they were still running around like chickens. So, I sat my butt down and waited for the ambulance.

"Are yall ready?" I asked laughing.

"Wait what are you doing down here?" Fuzz asked.

"I was waiting for you or G to come upstairs, but when you didn't I knew you was panicking. So, I got ready and called the ambulance." I laughed.

"Well here they come!"

9

"Hmm excuse me, can one of you headless chickens come and help me go outside."

'I am so sorry, let me grab your bag."

"I will be there as soon as I get dressed." Grace said.

"G, stay here with the kids. I will call you later. This baby is too early, and I am having no pain."

When we arrived at the hospital, my head was spinning. I sat in the wheel chair and they wheeled me to the Labor and Delivery Department. My heart was pounding while the intake nurse hooked me to the machine. She frowned and sucked her teeth as she tried to place the heart rate monitor for the baby.

"What's the matter?" I asked.

"I don't hear his heart beat," Fuzz started to panic. "What?"

"Let me call the doctor. Drink this while you wait." She gave me an orange juice.

As soon as I smelled it I threw up. Suddenly, a sharp pain rocketed across my belly. It felt like it caved in. I screamed, and Fuzz ran to the door. The doctor ran into the room and asked the nurse to check my pressure as he did a vaginal exam. My head was still spinning. I started to cry, praying that my baby was okay. Then, everything went black. When my eyes fluttered open again, I was in the operating room.

"What's happening?" I could only turn my head to see Fuzz sitting next to me.

"We are going to put you under now. Count to ten." The anesthesiologist told me as she placed a clear mask over my face.

They performed an emergency C-Section on me. Later, it was reported that our son's heart rate was about sixteen beats per minute. They thought he would be stillborn but by the grace of God he came out screaming. When I woke up though, Fuzz informed me that he was in the NICU. My heart sank as I looked at him with puffy eyes. He took my hand and leaned down to kiss my cheek.

"Is he going to be okay?"

"He had some fluid in his lungs. They aren't fully developed yet. And he has a feeding tube."

I felt like a failure. I had one job; to give birth to a healthy baby. I failed. Tears streamed down my face.

"Baby," said Fuzz, "it's going to be alright. He's going to be fine."

"Can I see him? I want to see my baby." I told him through the tears.

"They said they will come get us." He sat down in the chair next to me. I heard my phone ringing in the nearby closet. It was Drama; I could tell by the ringtone.

"Answer it. Tell her I will call her later. I don't feel like talking." I turned my head toward the other side of the room.

All I could do was cry. My baby had been born hours ago and I didn't know what he looked like. I hadn't held him or fed him. I didn't even know what his cry sounded like. Then, a doctor came into the room to explain the complications of my birth. I started to cry all over again. They told me that the baby was sick and that he would spend some time in the NICU. I would more than likely go home before him. It weighed heavy on me. If I wasn't so worried about the business and everyone else, my son would not be in the NICU. No matter what Fuzz said to console me, I cried. Partly because I was in pain and partially because I blamed myself. He wiped my tears. Then, he made a silts bath and pulled back the blanket. He pushed my legs back and started to clean me up.

I rested on the bed, thinking "This man really loves me." I smiled at that. He could have let the nurses do that part, but he had been there for me through all of this. Fuzz was the real MVP. A nurse came into the room and put me in a wheelchair, giving Fuzz the directions to the NICU.

Our son weighed two and a half pounds. He was so tiny with a blue light shining on him in the incubator. Despite all the tubes coming from his body, I was in love. It was unlike any feeling I had ever felt. My heart was full. I rubbed his little hand as more tears dropped from my eyes.

"Try skin to skin with him. It will help him get better." The nurse informed. She picked him up and placed him on my bare chest.

A mother's love is one no money could ever buy. I thought I wouldn't be cut out for this, but I loved my son instantly. I looked at Fuzz; amazed at the miracle we created. He wasn't out of the woods yet, but he was still perfect. He cooed and made sweet little noises as we stared at him in awe. He was my sweet little baby and he smelled good too.

Fuzz wheeled me back to the room and helped me into the bed. He leaned over me and kissed me on the forehead. I was glad that our baby was getting the help that he needed but I still felt guilty. My eyes were swollen from crying and I didn't have a lot of tears left. The nurse gave me a few pain pills to numb me, but it didn't stop what was going on in my head. In the distance, I could hear Mama's voice. I thought I told her I didn't want any visitors, I rolled my eyes. Fuzz eased out of the chair and addressed her at the door.

"Hey sis," he took the flowers from her hands as he kissed her on the cheek. "I don't…"

"No, it's okay." I spoke, rising the bed.

Mama came into the room with a big smile on her face. "Congratulations, sweet pea." She kissed me.

"Thank you," I forcefully smiled. "Where are the babies?"

"With Jodi." Mama sat down. "How's Little Fuzz?"

I laughed, "Don't call my baby that no more."

"Hey, hey…" Fuzz butted into the conversation, "what's wrong with that name? My grandma gave me that name."

I waved my hand at his sensitivity and the three of us shared a laugh. I tried not to laugh too hard because the stitches in my stomach hurt like hell. There was an IV in my hand too. They were administering an antibiotic for the infection that apparently caused all this mess. The doctor was careful to explain that none of this was my fault. Some babies decided on their own when they would come but his explanation didn't erase that while I was pregnant I hung around a few folks who smoked, I killed a couple of men, and ran a large drug cartel. My body was stressed, and my mind was exhausted. This was the price I was paying for being the Real Female Don Dada.

Trials and Tribulations

~Bev~

My momma used to tell me that Karma was a bitch. I remember a time when I smacked hellfire out of a bitch who was about six months pregnant. She didn't lose her child, but she fell hard on the ground. I didn't give to fucks and my right mind was telling me to stomp her ass out while she was down there.

It had been three weeks since I had given birth and my son was still in the NICU. Somedays it looked like he was getting better and others, he was sicker. His weight was fluctuating, and the doctors were unsure when he would be able to go home. Last week, he had to have surgery to repair his lung. His tiny body had gone through so much and I was convinced that it was all because of a bitch named Karma.

All the shit Fuzz and I had done was coming back and falling on our precious little son. Amid all this chaos, we hadn't given him a name. I wanted him to have a strong name, one that represented his resilience. There had been times when I thought my baby wasn't going to make it but he was continuing to prove me wrong. His name would be the first thing people learned about him and it had to be something that would resonate how much he means to Tracey and I.

Fuzz touched my shoulder and gave me a sweet smile. Small gestures, like that, went a long way these days. It seemed like I was living in my head. I didn't talk much and rarely slept. Hell, some days Fuzz had to force me to eat. I lost about ten pounds and my hair was a hot ass mess. Most nights, I laid in bed and cried. I wanted my son to be healthy enough to come home. This shit was pure torcher.

"He's going to be just fine. He's our son," Fuzz smiled.

"I know but it's easier said than done. He is cute though," I laughed.

"He got it from his daddy."

"How are things out there?" I changed the subject.

Fuzz looked around and said, "It's cool. Waiting on this work to come through. I got a few niggas I need to run down on but it ain't nothing major."

"It's always something major," I smacked my teeth.

"I don't know what the fuck Drama was out here in these streets doing but this shit is a mess." Fuzz shook his head.

"She wasn't ready," I sighed. "Poppa should have never let her run the throne in the first place. She was still a baby and now look?" I shook my head.

"Right, she fucked up and we out here picking up the pieces."

"We going to get the shit straight."

"You ain't got to worry about it, though. Take care of yourself and little man. I will handle the streets."

"I can always count on you." I reached for a kiss.

Mama told me that everything was going to be okay and that she had my back to the end, but I hadn't talked to her in a while. There was nothing to talk about. While my son was lying in the hospital, drugs and running things was the furthest from my mind. I knew that she loved me and wanted what was best for us, but her interest was in the money, no matter how much she wanted to say that she was out of the game. It was like they said, "you can take the girl out of the game, but you can't take the game out of the girl." If she wanted to show support, she could come clean my house or better yet, wash my hair.

I leaned forward in my seat and stroked the baby's hand.

"What are we going to name him?" I looked over at Fuzz.

"How about Aaron?" he asked. "It was my uncle's name."

14

"Aaron?" I repeated, and the baby wiggled. "I like that." I reached for a kiss.

That was one thing off the list. When we left to go to lunch, Fuzz filled me in on some of the things that were going on at the office. I was half listening to him, though. I was in my own world. I never believed it when my friends or family would talk about having postpartum depression. I thought it was just a cry for attention but now that I was going through it myself, I regretted ever ridiculing those women. It was hell. Worst for me, I was away from my baby. I couldn't take him home with me and somedays, I couldn't hold him. In the back of my mind, I was planning his funeral. I feared that one day I would wake up and my baby would be dead.

"What's the matter?" Fuzz touched my hand. "Are you okay?"

"I'm scared." I told him. "I just don't know anymore."

"Baby," he pulled her into a hug. "Maybe you need sometime. How about you go to the salon and get a makeover?" Fuzz suggested.

"But…"

"But nothing," he stood up and pulled my chair out. "Let's go."

It had been weeks since I smelled fresh cut grass. I watched the trees as he drove into downtown. Fuzz pulled a band from his wallet when he pulled up in front of the salon.

"I'll go sit with Aaron. Call me when you finished." He told me.

I kissed him on the cheek and climbed out of the car. I waved as he drove away. I was about to get the works done. I missed getting my hair and nails done. Fuzz was right, this was what I needed; something to get my mind off everything that was happening with Aaron. Being away didn't stop me from worrying though. I checked my phone every few minutes and even asked Fuzz to send me a few pictures of the baby.

The phone rang, and it was Drama. Finally, I answered her call.

"Are you mad at me or something?" she asked.

"No," I huffed. "I just have been going through something."

"I'm sorry. How is the baby?"

"We finally named him; Aaron." I smiled.

Suddenly my shirt was wet. I looked down and my nipples were leaking. I was embarrassed.

"You have baby?" the nail tech asked with a smile. "Me have baby, too."

"Yes. His name is Aaron. He's only a few weeks old."

It felt good to talk about my sweet baby boy to other people. It was the most I had smiled in weeks. As she finished with my nails, I couldn't wait to get back to the hospital. Drama was still on the phone, talking about something or another. I never noticed how long winded she could be until she got a life outside of hustling. I laughed in the middle of her statement and there was a brief silence on the phone.

"Hello?" Drama asked. "Are you laughing at me?"

"No, no. Just at your voice."

"My voice? Girl you silly!" Drama laughed. "I miss you, Bev."

"I miss you too. I'm sorry that I have been distant, but it's been hard."

"I know girl. If you need anything, don't hesitate to ask."

"I love you, boo. Fuzz is here to pick me up. I will call you when I leave the hospital."

"Okay." We hung up the phone.

~Fuzz~

I stepped into the rinky dink apartment and put a bag on the table. Charlette was sitting on one end with a joint dangling between her lips. She looked up at me with glassy eyes and snarled.

"I keep telling you bout bringing this mess up in my house, boy."

"Momma," I sighed and pulled a knot from my pocket, "here's a couple of dollars and a rock." I put it on the table and sat down to start sorting and bagging my drugs.

My phone rang. It was one of the shorties that hustled for us in her neighborhood. I told her to come through to pick up her weight. About twenty minutes later there was a knock on the door. I handed her a brown paper bag through the mail slot.

Momma was still sitting there, talking shit. She had been getting high since I was about two years old. My daddy introduced her to the pipe and they stayed together until he died in 08. By then I was making money selling the same shit she got happy off. So, I turned the apartment into the trap house and kept her quiet by suppling as much rock as she could smoke. I loved my Momma, but this was business.

When I was finished counting and sorting. I back peddled out of there and hopped in my car. The phone rung, it was my boy Puncho. He told me that he had some money I needed to put away, so I swung by his crib.

"What up, though?" Sandra answered the front door.

"What's Popping, blood?" I asked, passing her.

Puncho was sitting on the couch in his boxers, playing a round on his Xbox.

"What up, my boy?"

"Same, shit. Just a different day. You made your pickups?"

"Of course. But you know that nigga Brown be acting like he ain't got to pay up. Imma wind up murking that nigga for real."

"Chill," I laughed. "You can't be round here killing all our niggas off."

"Well," Puncho smacked his teeth. "You better check that lil nigga."

Me and Puncho went way back. He was one of the few niggas I trusted in the game. When I was down state, he was the only one flying kites and keeping a nigga books looking right. He never asked questions either. He just counted the money and made sure shit was right. It wasn't too bad that his woman was down with the shit too. She ran a couple of spots for us too. Sandra was a killer, though; thirsty as hell for blood and that's where she came in at.

After I left their spot, I picked Bev up from the salon. She wanted to go back to the hospital and sit with Aaron, but I convinced her to go home. I wanted to lay up with my baby for a while. It had been a long time since I held her in my arms. She needed that. I wished that I could take some of the pain out her eyes, but I knew that a mother's love was different than any other. She was never going to be the same after half the shit she'd been through.

I was supposed to be getting my life together and rolling out of the game. I knew a lot about the law, but I was going to ride for my shorty. Most of my best cases in Criminal Law came from the very niggas I ran with. I was ready to walk away but who was going to take care of my girl and my kid?

I have to do what I always knew how to do; hustle. I was trying my best but fast money was the root of my attraction. I could easily make six g's in a day while I'm out here in these streets. Putting on a suit and a tie to be in and out of a court room only gave me a few thousand a month. I wanted to conquer the fucking world. Bev was my ticket.

Her cake runs deeper than she knows. She is JR's daughter. There are some buried secrets that even Drama couldn't uncover. When the shit hits the fan, we'd all be some rich bitches. I was in it for that. I was going to stick by my wife's side. Then, there was the fact that I really do love her.

When It Rains, It Pours

~Fuzz~

The bedroom was quiet except for my phone. Bev was lightly snoring next to me. She was kind of cute when she was asleep. I couldn't fathom what could be so important at 3 in the morning. A part of me didn't want to answer the phone but I figured it had to be an emergency.

"Yo what the fuck?" I stirred in the bed and picked up my buzzing phone. "Niggas keep calling me and shit. It better be important." I pressed 'talk' and put the phone to my ear. "Hello?"

"Fuzz, this Puncho. Shit went south at the building."

"Man, the fuck?" I jumped up and started to put on my clothes. "I'm on my way."

Bev sat up in the bed and turned on the light. "What's the matter, Baby?"

"Go back to sleep." I went over to kiss her. "I will call you in a little while."

I grabbed my gun out of the closet and tossed on my bullet proof vest as I walked out of the door. Puncho called me again as I drove down the drive way, but I didn't answer. My mind was racing a mile a minute. I pulled up on his block and honked the horn. He ran out and hopped in the car.

"What happened?"

"So, I got a call that some West Side niggas hit our shit." He told me as the engine roared. "I'm ready to blast all these niggas!" Puncho revealed a hand riffle and two other guns.

There had been an ongoing feud between us and the West Side. Our supply was better, simply put. Them niggas was mad that their customers would rather walk across town for an eight ball. I wasn't with the stick-up shit and mother fuckers was going to have to learn the hard way not to fuck with my territory. Shit could get real ugly, real quick. It wasn't shit for me to split a nigga wig open, right where he stood. As a matter of fact, that shit gave me a rush—probably why Bev married me.

We reached the West Side projects, where the neighborhood was practically empty. The cement was still wet from the rain and it was so quiet that you could hear a mouse piss on cotton. I turned my lights off and slowly drove down one of the dark alleys. I cocked back the gun that was snuggly in my lap when I saw a group of thugs. I heard them shout a code and start to scatter. That cued Puncho and I to bust off in every direction. One of them dropped to the ground with a loud thud. I hopped out of the car and ran up to him with my heat still drawn. He was rolling around on the ground, holding his leg in pain.

"Who sent y'all coward ass niggas to my spot?" I asked, aiming at his head.

"Nigga…" the young boy hissed and pain, "kiss my ass."

"Oh, you wanna act tough." I wrapped my finger around the trigger.

As I started to pull it, I heard a loud pop and felt a burning sensation in my back. Rapidly, their gunfire rang in the air. Puncho was busting back but I had already been hit. I tried hard to pull myself back to the bullet riddled car.

"Let's get the fuck out of here." I shouted to Puncho, who was huffing in the distance.

"Damn, man!" he screeched, pushing me into the back seat of the car.

"Fuccckkkk!" I screamed loudly, clutching the many wounds that leaked blood.

Puncho was speeding toward the nearest hospital. I was in the backseat of my car, bleeding all over the place. I could barely breathe but I pulled out my phone and called Bev. I tried to tell her that I loved her, but she was screaming on the other end of the phone.

"What happened?" she cried.

"We are going.... we are going..." Then, things went black.

***

~Bev~

Oh, my god, I scrambled to put on my clothes, holding the phone between my shoulder and face. Mama answered the phone quickly and I told her that something happened to Fuzz. She said that she would meet me at the hospital but at the point, I didn't even know what hospital he was in. Thinking quickly, I pulled up the GPS history of his phone and learned that he was on the Westside. Then, I hopped in my car and sped toward the hospital. My mind was racing, and I couldn't think straight. I could remember that Avant and Keke Wyatt song playing on the radio as I parked the car in front of the hospital. My heart was in the pit of my stomach when I saw Fuzz's car blocking the main entrance. It was lit with bullets and the driver's and back door was wide open.

I ran into the hospital and to the security guard. "My husband, he was brought here from that car outside..." I pointed to the door. "Where is he? Is he okay?" I was balling with tears and fear. "Please, tell me where he is."

"Ma'am," she said, calmly, "please calm down."

"No, bitch!" I raged. "You calm down. Where is he?"

"Trauma unit. That way." She shrugged her shoulders.

I was getting ready to curse her out but finding out what was going on with Fuzz was more important. The trauma unit was crowded with cops.

"What the fuck?" I whispered to myself.

Then, I saw Fuzz. He was sprawled out on a table with his shirt ripped open. There were IV's hooked to him and a doctor standing over him. I couldn't see what they were doing but it didn't look like he was conscious. Tears were running down my cheeks. Suddenly, someone tapped me on the shoulder.

"Sis..." it was Puncho.

21

"What happened?" I asked him. "What did they do to my baby?"

He pulled me into a hug and I cried on his shoulder. I heard the doctors screaming a code and yelling for an operating room. They whisked Fuzz off. My heart couldn't take it. I sat down on the floor and cried while Puncho tried to hold me. Mama showed up at the hospital while we sat in the waiting room.

A doctor stepped into the hallway, blood covering his chest area. He didn't have to say it, I knew Fuzz was dead. He lowered his head in sorrow as he approached us.

"He had been shot several times. Some of the bullets went through and through. It was touch and go for a while, but he is alive."

"He's alive?" I asked with wide eyes and lofty expectations.

"He's in a medically induced coma and he's not out of the woods yet."

"Can I see him?" I asked.

"Someone will come get you when they finish up in the operating room." The doctor walked away.

Tragedy always had a way of weaseling its way into my life. First Aaron and now, Fuzz. What more can I take? I wasn't perfect, no one is, but when will all this stop. I sat in the waiting room for about two more hours before someone came to take me to see Fuzz. There was a cop standing at the door and when I opened it, Fuzz was chained to the bed. I frowned, wanting to know why but I didn't ask. His face was swollen, and a machine was breathing for him. He looked completely hopeless, but he was strong, so I knew he would come back to me. I replayed the call he had placed to me earlier. I wished that I had a chance to tell him that I loved him.

I kissed him on the forehead and rubbed his hand, praying that he would survive. Puncho came into the room with his own set of regrets.

"I should have gone to check on them niggas myself." He said from across the room.

"There's nothing you could have done about this." I reminded him.

"My boy…" A lone tear drizzled down his face. "My fucking boy."

"Don't do that to yourself. He's going to be just fine."

"I hope so." Puncho lowered his head.

Sandra wrapped her arms around Puncho and I sat there, rocking back and forth. My mind was on revenge. First the niggas had the nerve to run up in my spot but now, they shot my man. Something was fixing to go down and everyone in this town was going to know my name. My face was starting to get hot and my hands were shaking. I let out a loud scream. Frustration was getting the best of me.

"Wanna go for a walk, sis?" Sandra asked.

"I guess." I told her, unsure of my next move.

The cold air hitting my face was enough to bring me down for a while. "Sis, I ain't going to rest til I get answers. Who out here robbing my spots? This hasn't been the first time since Drama got knocked. It's got to be somebody in my camp."

"Do you really think so?" Sandra asked with wide eyes. "You have instilled your trust in them."

"Trust is nothing but a word in this game." I told her. "I don't even trust my own Momma."

Sandra pulled out a pack of cigarettes, offering me one. I hadn't smoked since I was pregnant with Aaron, so I took one and lit it.

"I don't know what I will do if I lose Tracey. It's been me and him for so long. We have a son. Our son is up there," I looked toward the hospital, "fighting for his life while his daddy is down here fighting for his."

"Sis, it's going to be okay."

"No. It ain't. I done did a lot of shit to a lot of people, Sandra. God ain't gonna look out for me?" Tears weld up in my eyes.

"I ain't never seen you like this before." Sandra wrapped her arms around me.

23

My world was crashing down before me. I haven't suffered a hard lost in a long time. I was young when Murda killed my father, but I remember sitting in the back row at his funeral. My Momma told me not to say anything to anyone because no one knew who we were. He was good to me, that's what I remember. I took it hard when he was killed and since then, I have been searching for a man to love me that way JR had. I went through a couple of crabs and then, I found Tracey. He had my heart the moment we met.

He was a street dude with a lot of sex appeal. We had sex the first night we met and every night after that. He reminded me so much of my father—slinging coke and busting guns. Whatever I asked him for, he gave me; including the opportunity to meet Grace. I will be grateful to him for that and my son forever. I can't imagine my life without my baby.

From Dreams to Nightmares

It was around four thirty in the morning when the phone rang. I had a habit of keeping the ringer loud in case a doctor called for either Aaron or Fuzz. I reached over and pressed it to my ear.

"Hello, this is Nurse Annabelle calling regarding Tracey Fields."

I sat up in bed; she was calling about Fuzz. "Yes?" I answered, hesitantly.

"He's awake and he's been asking about his son and wife." She told me.

"Oh, my god!" I flipped the cover back and turned on the light.

"Visiting hours start at eight and I am sure he will want to see you all."

"Thank you so much for calling!" I hung up the phone.

I couldn't contain myself. I got up and started to take out what I would be wearing to go see my boo. He had been in a coma for a week and I had to look good for him. I had a few hours to get ready too. I called his mother and let her know the good news. She sounded like she had just come out of a coma herself. She was a crack head and didn't really care if her son was dead or alive as long as she had a crack rock. I asked Fuzz to put her in a rehab, but he has accepted the fact that nothing was ever going to change his momma. She wasn't willing to change, either. I smacked my teeth and hung up the phone when she asked if I could bring her an eight ball. In my book, it was always about the green. Momma or no Momma she had to pay, and I definitely wasn't dropping it off for free.

I arrived at the hospital around eight thirty. I was anxious to see Fuzz as the elevator rode up to the six floor. It was the Intensive Care Unit. He must have been strong to have survived being shot seven times. They'd performed three surgeries on him in the past week as well. I was certain he would look a hot mess when I walked into the room.

Some of the swelling in his face had finally gone down. I smiled at him when I entered the room. I was draped in a tight black dress with a pair of red pumps. I leaned over and kissed him on the cheek. He had the blanket over his wrist as if I didn't know that he was chained to the bed.

"So, what happened?" I asked him.

"I don't remember." He told me. "All I know is I woke up chained to the bed. The cops ain't even come in here yet." He looked at the door. "All I know is Puncho called me and said someone hit our spot."

"Hit our spot?" I frowned. "Which one?"

"He said the building; didn't you go check it out?"

"Puncho never told me what happened."

"Maybe he was just mixed up in all that was happening with me."

"How they shoot you seven times and he didn't catch one bullet?"

Something didn't sound right. Puncho was reluctant to tell me that he was the one who called Fuzz in the first place and he damn sure failed to mention that any of our spots had taken a loss. I was down for being loyal to your friends, but how could he leave me in the wind like that. I visited the Building several times since this incident and didn't notice anything out of place. Perhaps Fuzz heard him wrong.

"I don't know, baby. He was there, busting his shit too. I don't even know if he hit one of the niggas, either." Fuzz snapped his teeth.

"Nah, Blood." I shook my head. "I'ma get to the bottom of this shit."

"What's up?" Fuzz frowned. "You think that nigga set me up?"

"I don't know. That's ya boy. He could have though." I shook my head. "Sandra ass seemed eager to talk to me too."

"Nah, you can't possibly think she in on the shit too."

I thought about it for a moment. It made sense. Some one that was on the inside of my empire was fucking us over. They were both here that night. Things were adding up. But why? I gave both they asses a place to lay. I was praying that the betrayal wasn't that deep, but you better believe I'ma make they asses put in work before they make a fool of me.

Two detectives walked into the room. "I'm Detective Perry and this is my partner, Detective Singleton. We are here conducting a murder investigation."

"Murder investigation? My husband was shot in the street."

"That we understand but a seventeen-year-old boy was shot in the head with a gun that was found in the parking lot with your husband's finger prints on it."

"I was there at the scene of the crime," Tracey told him, "but I didn't mean to hurt anyone. I am a lawyer. I was there to see my client when gun fire erupted."

"And you shot and killed a young man?"

"Yes, he shot at me. I shot my licensed fire arm."

"If your story doesn't check out, we will be back." The detectives left but Fuzz was still confined to the bed.

"Have the doctors come in to talk to you?" I asked him with concern in my eyes.

"I'm never going to walk again, huh?"

"God has all the power." I told him.

Tracey smacked his teeth. "God? What in the hell you know about God? I'm up in here in all this pain and you want to talk to me about God?"

"Baby," I said, calmly. "I don't want to upset you."

I could see the pain and anger in his eyes. I didn't want to upset him any farther, so I picked up my purse and looped my arm in it. My mind was in ten places. I wanted to know what Puncho and Sandra had to do with all of this. I swear to God if I find out that they're playing for the other team it's a fucking wrap.

When Drama had put Sandra on the team, I was against it. She seemed a little off to me. She was six feet tall with big feet and big hands, but her voice sounded like a baby's. She would always prance around in tight dresses but when it was time to kill, she was there with a smoking gun. I had watched her shoot three niggas without letting go of the trigger. She was a fucking beast. So, after a while she grew on me and had become like a big sister. A part of me was praying that noon of the shit was true though.

"I'm leaving." I started to walk away but he hissed.

"Don't leave me, Beverly. I need you." He whimpered. "That's how we are doing it, now?"

"Tracey," I started through clenched teeth. "We been through hell and back together and now that I am trying to act like your wife…"

"Act like my wife?" he frowned.

I snapped my teeth, "You know what I mean. Fuzz, I'm pissed at you." I pouted.

"I know, baby." He sighed. "And I am sorry I put you through all of this. But I need you, right now." He sounded so pitiful.

I stood there, frozen. It was the first time he sounded so weak. He sounded as if he *did* need me. I knew that he was feeling inadequate. He had been told that he'd never walk again. He would never be able to play football with our son or bust a gun again. Who was going to protect his family if he couldn't walk? I hadn't even thought about the possibilities of him spending time in prison. The thought of that scared me more.

I turned to him with tears in my eyes, "Promise to never talk to me like that again."

"I promise. I'm sorry baby."

"I bet you are," I smirked.

I sat down at his bed side and showed him pictures of Aaron. He was getting bigger and better. The doctors told me that he would be able to come home soon. I was relieved by that news, but it only meant that I would be bringing him here to see Fuzz. It couldn't get any worse than this. I was glad that the detectives hadn't arrested him, though.

I left the hospital visit a few hours later, still combing through the information that Fuzz had revealed. Why didn't one of them tell me that Puncho called Fuzz that night? Shit was heavy, now. I was out for blood. I got into the car and called G.

"Meet me at the building." I told him and hung up.

G was standing near the front entrance of the building when I pulled up. He opened my car door and helped me out. He was standing there with his chocolate ass, looking like a damn Hershey's bar. I was about to take my panties off and hand them to him, but I smiled, instead.

"You're looking beautiful as always."

"Flattering." I smiled. "You know Fuzz going to kick your ass if he finds out you are flirting with me."

"How? He can't walk." G snarled.

"The fuck?" I frowned and shook my head. "That was some cold-hearted shit to say."

"What? It's the truth."

I wanted to laugh but I was optimistic about him being paralyzed. I followed G into the building and started to tell him what Fuzz told me. He agreed the shit sounded suspect.

If it was one thing that had never changed about G, it was his mouth. He had been that way since we were in junior high. He was a quiet kid, taller than the average eighth grader and he had a deep ass voice. Sometimes the other kids would pick on him and steal his lunch money. I would find him in the back of the library, hiding. One day, I walked up to him and asked what the matter.

"Yo, I cannot keep hiding back here, huh?" he asked with big eyes as I handed him a sandwich.

"No. Niggas starting to think you a pussy." I laughed.

That day, Gene squared up with a dude from PS 113 in the parking lot. They were going toe to toe until a teacher broke it up. G had broke the boy's jaw in two places. He never feared another nigga after that day. We been rolling since. He was my boy and Fuzz had accepted him as a best friend, too.

I sat down behind my desk and crossed my legs. My jaw was tight, and a vein was bulging from my forehead. I was getting ready to explode.

"Sandra and Puncho was down with this shit," I looked at G.

"They had something to do with it. Now, what do you want to do about it?" He asked.

I leaned back in my chair and folded my hands in my lap. "I don't know, yet. But I wanna make the shit hurt."

"You know, I'm with whatever, your fine ass wanna do."

"Oh, stop it, G."

"I love the way you say my name."

"So childish." I laughed at his antic.

29

"You love my childish ways. You think it's sexy, right?" he walked around the desk and leaned over me in the seat.

I looked up at him and batted my eyes. "As long as it comes with a dollar sign."

G frowned and stood up. Perplexed by my comment he asked, "So, it's like that?"

"Any nigga whose name is not Tracey Fields has to pay for this sweet pussy." I taunted.

He tugged at his suite jacket and took his seat. "We'll see about that. My money long. Name your price."

I shot him a crazed look and burst into laughter. "You crazy ass hell." I pulled my chair up and turned on the computer to order a meeting with all my guys. Somebody was playing and if that meant I had to bring out the big guns to get to the bottom of it then so be it.

Today, they will learn that my camp isn't one to be played with. The guys sat around the table and started to polish our weapons.

"So, let's clear up one mother fucking thing," I snarled from my seat at the table, "my team is not one to be fucking played with. There will be hell to pay for whoever lured Fuzz to the projects. This war is getting out of hand. Y'all only job is to make money and kill who ever stands in the way of us getting it. I thought I told yall niggas, I ain't Drama. Yall need to tighten the fuck up!"

"Boss Lady," Dough Boy spoke, "there wasn't no hit on none of our shit though."

I cut my eye at him, "I know so...."

"Word on the streets is," Sandra sashayed into the room—interrupting what I was about to say—and put her purse on the table, "Sweets is the one who ordered the hit."

Is this bitch out of her fucking mind. My left hand was twitching. G leaned over, putting his hand on top of mine, and whispered, "Chill."

I leaned back in my chair and listened to this bitch lie through her teeth. Who was telling her all of this shit if it wasn't the people in her head. I sucked my teeth thinking that I should off her ass right there, but I knew it would be too soon. Either Puncho was full of shit or they thought I was boo -boo the fucking fool. Either way, someone would be dead when it was all said and done.

Sandra thought she had shit in the bag but if she keeps playing with me, she going to be in the bag. I rolled my eyes at her so hard that if looks could kill, she would be dead. I stared at her, remembering something my mother had taught me, *never eat steak with snakes*. I knew when Drama put her ass on that she was no good, there is something about her demeanor that really gets under my skin; she ain't for the team.

I went along with the show, though. "I want his head on a fucking platter. Fuzz is still in the ICU and these pigs done locked him up. We have to do something before they think they can destroy us." I told them. "Now," I turned to my sexy decoy, Sandra, "you know how all this works, right?" I asked her with a smirk.

"Yes," she smiled back. "Sweet pussy."

***

~Sandra~

A purple leather dress kissed my hips and my thighs as my heels click clacked on the glossy floors of the Hot Cheetah Gentlemen's Club. I wore a painted-on smile as I sat down at the bar.

It was owned by a man named Sweets, except he wasn't all that sweet. He was tall, bald, and stocky. He reminded me of Mr. Clean. Since the early 90's he and his boys had control of most of the Westside. They sold more drugs than the Italian Mob. I'm talking pure cocaine. I had a personal vendetta with the ugly ass man because it was his crack rock that had gotten my momma hooked. As much as I would have liked to blame that shit on her own stupidity, it gave me more ammunition to want to kill him.

Through a little bit of research, I found out that he was the one who had ordered the hit on Bev's Empire. So, I was ready to reel him in like a fish on a hook. I sat at the bar with my legs crossed at the knee. The bartender strolled over and asked what I would like.

"A blue Long Island." I told her.

When she sat the drink in front of me, I took a slow sip and scanned the room. Sweets was a show off type of nigga so I knew he was in the club somewhere, trying to cop a feel. My intuition was right. He was on the other side of the room, hugged up with some broad. I slid off the bar stool, drink in hand, and stood in front of him. His eyes fell on me and he smiled.

"I know you from somewhere." He said in a thick Jamaican accent.

"I bet you do." I shrugged my shoulder. "I saw you from across the room and my panties got wet."

"Is that so?" he removed his arm from around the girl's neck and licked his lips.

I put my hand under my dress and wiggled out of the thong I was wearing. A nasty look came on to his face as I put it in his hand. The girl rolled her eyes and walked away.

"So, you tryna go somewhere more private, huh?"

"If you wanna lick this sweet pussy." I walked off and he followed me.

I wasn't the type of girl to play a lot of games. When I wanted something, I was going to get it. Sure, Bev said that she wanted his head on a platter, but not until I get mines. Sweets couldn't wait to close the door of his office and lay me down on the desk. My dress was hiked up over my hips and he was kissing me all over my neck. His breath smelled like rum and the palms of his hands felt like sand paper. I held my breath until he put his finger in my pussy.

"Wait," I moaned.

"What's the matter?" he asked.

32

"You have to pay first."

"Pay," he laughed. "Girl, I get free pussy anywhere."

"Well, not today." I huffed.

"Girl get your ass on…." He shouted. I didn't budge though. "I said…"

"Lemma suck ya dick, then you pay." I smiled.

He eased up and started to unbuckle his pants. I got down on my knees and took his little dick into my mouth. It was a poor little thing, too. I sucked and slurped along with his balls. He was yanking at the back of my head and begging me to stop.

"Okay, okay. I will pay." He pulled away and pulled a wad of bills out of his pocket. Pulling off fifteen hundred, he pushed me back on the desk.

He put his little dick into my slippery pussy and pounded as if pussy was going out of style. I moaned and groaned, trying to convince him that it was the best dick I ever had. He came quick and I rolled off the desk.

"See you next week." I switched out of the room.

He didn't know my name, but he didn't care. I was going to put him under a spell and the rest would be history. Bev would be so proud when I come rolling into the building with Sweets following like a lost pup. I laughed as I got into my car and drove home.

You Could Hate Me Now

~Bev~

"Bag this shit up," I barked, walking around the round table of workers.

The table was piled high with coke and drug paraphernalia. Both men and women packed nickel, dime, and quarter bags of coke and dope while some cooked and weighed it. It was a system that allowed me to watch what was coming in and what was going out. I wore a face mask to prevent inhaling the fumes. I couldn't risk contaminating the breastmilk I fed Aaron.

The workers didn't look up. They were naked, except for the scarves that covered their faces. My eyes darted from one end of the room to the other. G and Puncho stood in either of the opposite corners of the room to keep an extra watchful eye. The workers knew that if they decided to steal from me, that there would be heavy consequences.

When they finished bagging the drugs, G and Puncho helped them pack it into boxes, which we would deliver to several street runners around town. They piled the drugs into our cars. Then, G and I got into my car while Puncho and one of the others got into his.

G and I stopped by the nearest house first. It was a rundown row house in a housing complex called Banks Housing. He parked the car in front of the house and I stepped out in a grey pants suit with a badge attached to the breast pocket. The boys on the porch nodded at me, believing that I was a parole officer. I smiled and rang the doorbell, package in hand.

"Good afternoon, Mr. Caldwell," I said, loud enough for them to hear. "Can I come in? I hope that you have been behaving yourself." I smiled.

"I have," he let me in and closed the door. "So, what do you have for me today?"

"A generous offer." I placed the five-pound box on the table and opened it with a razor.

Mr. Caldwell's eyebrow raised on his forehead and he took one of the small packets, holding it up to the light. He licked his lips and opened the package. Then, he took a long sniff.

"This is good, Beverly." He smiled at me.

He backed up, without taking his eyes off me, and picked up a briefcase. "And I have something for you." He told me, opening it.

"Bev, we have been having some trouble with some of the runners. What do you think that we should do about it?" He asked

"What kind of trouble?" I asked sitting down.

"Well missing money and drugs. People hanging around that shouldn't be there. And just mad respect when I say something about it." He stated.

"Well listen, this is your crew. If they are coming up with missing stuff, I would dead them no questions asked. And as far as disrespect. Once you allow it, you will never get it back. The people hanging around, that's a set up. My advice to you is this. Get it under control, before I have to ghost you for messing with my money. Do I make myself clear?" I said standing turning my attention back to the briefcase.

It was lined with hundred-dollar bills. I took the briefcase and left the drugs on the table. As I walked out the same dudes were standing there staring at me. I felt a little twinge run down my spine. I quickly pulled back my suit jacket to flash my piece and smiled at them. Dropping the holster latch off, I slid the safety off and smiled again as I continued to walk down the stairs. When I got back into the car, G backed out of the parking spot and headed to the next drop off spot. We handled most of our drop offs the same way. After collecting all the money, we met back at the building.

Sandra told me that she had a meeting with Sweets that night. We were a little bit closer to catching our mark, but I really needed her to act faster. I couldn't risk my spot getting hit again. Fuzz wasn't there to protect me anymore and if I had to get out there and solve some problems myself, I risked losing Aaron.

Because of the shooting, Fuzz was paralyzed from the waist down but that didn't stop the pigs from putting him behind bars for the murder of that boy. Crazy as it is, that shit happens out here all the time. There were thousands of unsolved murders of black men, but Fuzz was in jail. I hated it. Why was he the one to get caught. I know it sounds selfish as fuck but if he hadn't gotten shot, he would be right here beside me.

I closed the building and went to the hospital to see Aaron. He was gaining weight and doing so much better. I pulled up a chair beside his bed and he smiled at me as he opened his eyes. His bassinet was crowded with pictures of the family. I wanted him to know that he was loved. My baby boy would be coming home soon, I hoped.

***

"Ayo, Bev." Puncho said into the phone.

"What up?" I asked him, settling down on the couch.

"Turn on the TV," he ordered.

"For what?" I frowned.

"Just do it." He told me.

I wasn't too beat for the games, so I smacked my teeth but did what he said. A video popped up. It was Fuzz. He was sitting at a table in a green jump suit. Even in the wheel chair and behind the wall, my man still looked good. I smiled, seeing his handsome face made me smile.

"Hey, baby girl. I wanted to shoot you this kite to let you know how ya man was doing up in here. I know it been a while since we saw each other but these niggas treating me aight in here. You see, I'm gaining weight and shit, right. Anyway, girl, you know I love you and my baby boy. Kiss him for me and tell him that Daddy will be home soon."

"Home soon?" I asked aloud.

"Yea," Poncho's raspy voice said on the phone. "Due to shitty evidence and shady police work, the state has dropped the case."

"You are lying."

"Never, Ma." She heard Fuzz's voice.

What the...I turned around and he wheeled himself into the room. I dropped the phone and ran into his out stretched arms. This shit had to be a dream. Just last week, the lawyer was telling him he could be facing five to ten years in prison and now, he was in our house.

"I can't believe it," I cried. "I really can't."

"Daddy's home baby girl."

"So, they just let you go?"

There had to be more to the story. It was just too good to be true. I watched enough true crime shows to know that he wasn't let off the hook like this. Something was amiss, he wasn't telling the whole truth. I wasn't going to question it right then, though. He was home, now. It was all that I had been praying for. The icing on this cake would be to have Aaron home too. It was just wishful thinking though.

Fuzz climbed from the wheelchair and into the bed and asked me to sit next to him. At first, I was nervous because he had a colostomy bag. That would be the total worst; if that shit burst. LITERALLY. I thought, lying back on the bed.

"Girl, I ain't going to bite you." He laughed. "Unless you want me too."

"Boy, please. You ain't in no condition to be trying to bite nobody, now." I shoved him.

Fuzz sucked his teeth, "You crazy as hell," he grabbed his harden cock, "I will shove this shit so far down your throat all you will be able to say is, 'Hotdog?'."

I laughed. I had really missed him. "Shut up."

He was the same clown that left me, then. He was laughing and joking but I was still scared as fuck to touch him. Everything was different, and I knew that whatever he did to get out was going to come back and haunt us.

The next morning, Fuzz came with me to the building. Sandra was there, telling me that tonight might have been the night that she brought me Sweets. I was smiling from ear to ear, knowing that it would have made Fuzz very proud.

"No," he interjected in her boast.

Sandra stared at him blankly. "But he was the one who sent..."

"Bev, tell her ass to shut up and listen." Fuzz rolled his eyes.

I didn't say anything, and Sandra gasped but obliged. "Okay," she threw her hands up.

"I want this nigga myself. He tried to have me done in but he is going to have to face me."

"What you talking about?" I frowned.

"He sent them mother fuckers to rob us, Bev. Not only that, niggas in our camp think they can get away with working for the other man?" Fuzz cut his eyes at Sandra.

I was dumbfounded. What did that have to do with Sweets? Fuzz shook his head and snapped his teeth.

"Huh?" she stared at him.

"Your pretty dick ass ain't got to worry about it."

"The hell are you talking about? It must be them perc's you taking, or some shit, got you talking crazy." I stood up. "Look, Sandra, bring me the nigga when you see fit. I need to go see my son."

I started to walk out of the office when

"The nigga copped some blow from me a while back, right?"

I nodded my head, still trying to put two and two together. Sweets ran a fairly large cartel himself. Why the hell would he be buying from Fuzz? I'm listening to the story thinking; this nigga was out here making bad deals while I was laid up having our kid. A part of me wanted to smack the shit out of his limp dick, shit bag having ass, but I was trying to keep my cool.

"He also brought a gun, one like the one I shot the little nigga with. He set me up."

"All this shit sound stupid as hell. He the fucking enemy, why you are trusting him with anything?" I snarled.

"Chill out, Bev." Fuzz raised his hand. "There's always a method with my madness."

"Nah, fuck all that shit. Your story sound crazy as hell. And frankly, I ain't here for the shit. Sandra, you know what to do." I stood up and walked away.

It wasn't like his handy capped ass could chase me. I went into my office and closed the door. I wasn't sure if I believed the bullshit Fuzz was trying to feed me, but I knew that one way or the other, I wanted Sweets' head on a platter. Sandra was going to deliver, and I would be the one to shoot that nigga right between the eyes. Between me and you, as soon as I figure out what the fuck Fuzz and Puncho's ass is up to, I will off they asses, too, if need be.

I wasn't the type of bitch either of them wanted to play with. I tooted guns and I was not afraid to use them. Drama had taught me well. I wanted to make sure that my name and my empire was never compromised again. It was business, nothing personal. I was not about to make the same mistakes that Drama made. I was not going to give people the chance to infiltrate and betray me. I love my husband, but he needed to tell me something and quick. Drama fell in love with a fuck boy, but I would be damned if I did. All this secret shit he was doing was not about to fly with me. I remember the signs that Drama missed as I reminisced about the conversation that I had with her...

"D, I know that you love Marquis. But why do you trust him so much?" I asked.

"I have been through a lot and Mama Mabel approved of him when she met him. She has never steered me wrong. So, I trust him."

"I understand your trust in Mama Mable's opinion. But she reminds me of a person that lives by the credo, "Keep your friend close and your enemies closer." Maybe you need to take heed to that. Something is not right. I don't like how he has been moving lately." I said.

"Do you really think that I need to pay attention?" She asked.

"Yes, and I really think that you need to clarify with Mama why she trusts him." I added.

"Let me ask you, why are you so concerned?" She asked with a raised eyebrow.

"Because your family. You have been there for me. And the least I could do is be there for you. If I notice something is not right, and I don't say something. Then I am a part of the problem and someone that you don't need to trust. I am not that person and never will be. I am a friend and always will be." I stated.

"I will talk to Mama then." She said.

I am glad that I had that talk with her, but I wish it came sooner. Because of that, I vowed that no one not even the man I loved would ever betray me. My eyes would stay open.

First Things First

Bev

Fuzz laid in the bed next to me, typing something on his phone. It took everything in me not to snatch that shit out of his hand. I was trying to be patient, but he was making my ass itch with all the lies and stalling. He had a few connects with lawyers and judges but now, I wasn't sure if he was on my side or nah. Why the hell is he out, strolling free, but Drama was still sleeping in a 10x10. I wasn't for the shit and he was going to have to give me some answers.

"Why you staring at me?" He asked.

"Why you lying to me?" I retorted.

Fuzz sighed and put his phone on the counter. He scooted up in the bed and turned his head toward me. Looking me square in the eyes he asked, "Do you trust me?"

"Not really."

He frowned as if I was talking in a foreign language. I wasn't going to sit here and lie to him. I didn't trust him as far as I could throw him. Frankly, the only reason he was still sleeping in my bed was Aaron. He was the only thing that connected us.

I met Fuzz when I was fifteen. He taught me a lot about the game but especially about myself. His ways helped me learn what I would and would not take from a nigga. He was smart, streetwise and book wise.

He went to an ivy league school on a debate scholarship. Most of the niggas from our hood were dead before twenty and if they went to college it wasn't because they were smart it was because of how high they could jump. To say the least, I was proud of Fuzz and even prouder to say that he was my man. But I knew the real him. The nigga that haunted drug dealers like lion food. I knew the man that pushed more coke and dope than Frank Lucas. He was more attractive to me than the man who stood in front of a judge and got his street pushers off. I wanted the thug. For a few years, he gave me that. Shooting up liquor stores and robbing niggas for their chains, Fuzz was a no-nonsense cheating thug. He made a couple of babies in between too. So, when he finally introduced me to Drama, he vowed that he would change his ways. He did and this time, I wasn't worried about another bitch, I was pressed about him playing for the other team. He was looking more and more like one of thing. I was praying that wasn't the case. I was hoping that he was just trying to help me conquer the world. If I found out that he was indeed against me, there will be hell to pay.

"I promise," Fuzz pulled my face into his, "I'm going to make this right and then, you will understand what it's all about. You my wife, right? Till death do us part? My rider?"

I kissed his lips, wanting to believe him so badly but I was more convinced that he wasn't being loyal. If there was anything Drama's relationship with Marquis taught me, it was that none of these niggas could be trusted.

My phone rang, and Sandra's name was flashing on the screen. I clicked 'talk' and pressed it to my ear.

"What up?" I asked, climbing out of the bed and going into the bathroom.

I closed the door and sat on the edge of the tub with my legs folded at the knee. I was waiting for her to say that she was ready to bring me Sweets. I already knew how I wanted to handle him.

"So, he asked me to go on a trip with him to Jamaica" She said.

I rolled my eyes and smacked my teeth; clearly agitated. "And what does this have to do with me?"

41

"Everything. He ain't going there for pleasure. This is business. If I go, I can find out who his dealer is."

I was listening but the only thing I saw was blood. I just wanted to kill him and get it over with, but Sandra was dragging the shit out. It almost made me look at her sideways too.

Then she said, "The supplier is key in taking his empire down. No more drugs, no more business."

I was thinking about it. "Okay," I said finally. "Go with him."

"Yes, sis, yes." She exclaimed excitedly.

I laughed and told her to call me before they left.

-Sandra-

After hanging up the phone, I confirmed that I would go with Sweets to Jamaica. He was such a sucker for this pussy. He called me at least three times a day and for the right price I sucked his dick until he squirted on my face. My passport had a few stamps, but this would be the first for Jamaica. While collecting information, I will be having a wonderful time on his dime.

I started to pack and sat down on the edge of the bed. Looking over my shoulder when Puncho stirred in the bed, I greeted him with a warm smile.

"What's up, baby? Where you are going?" He asked. I sucked my teeth and sighed, "Too handle some business for Bev."

"When is this shit going to end?" He asked, swinging his milk chocolate legs over the edge of the bed. "You out here fucking and taking flights."

"I know, baby. But we got bills to pay. This shit paying me more than Fuzz ass paying you, so I got to do what I got to do."

"Yea and when they find out the truth, you and I might both be dead...." He mumbled.

"Nah, we going to be living on the beach." I straddled his lap. "You know I love you baby and I'm doing this for us."

"I guess. I'm ready for the shit to be over though." He rubbed my thigh.

"I have to tie up some loose ends and pay the rest of the bill for the surgery; then, we out. Trust me."

I stood in front of the mirror, staring at my store brought body. My tittes cost over five thousand and my pussy more than twenty-five grand. But it was worth it. Puncho didn't seem to mind when I told him that I was born a man. That's probably why he trusted me to help him carry out his mission against Fuzz. He knew that I was strong enough to handle my business.

To tell the truth, I felt bad for Bev. She could potentially get caught in the crossfire of all of this. I was starting to like her, I was starting to grow a soft spot for her. I thought of her and Drama as my little sisters. They were just two girls trying to make it in a male dominated game. I wanted to help them—make sure they stayed on top but when it was all said and done, my loyalty was to my man.

Puncho and I had met a few years back at the casino. I was out in Atlantic City fucking up some commas when a fine tall bronze man walked up beside me. He licked his full lips as he shoved his card into the machine.

"Good luck." I told him, pressing a button on the machine in front of me.

He chuckled and placed his bid. After a couple of spins, he hit about five hundred.

"Shit you must be good luck because I ain't won shit til I sat next to you."

"Oh really?" I sized him up.

He was wearing a pair of blue jeans, an Adidas jacket, and a fresh pair of Tims. He looked like he had a couple of dollars but then again, niggas put on when they go out. I tooted up my lips and thought; ah what the hell?

"Yea. What's your name?"

"Sandra," I told him. "You?"

"Puncho." He said shyly.

It was something about him. He was different from the guys I usually ran into. He looked like had some humility, a heart. He was probably fresh from a bid or something but the look in his eyes was sincere.

Back then, I was just starting my transformation. I wore my hair in a bob and I had just got my boobs done. If you didn't ask, though, or have a high gaydar, you would have assumed I was a woman.

Puncho looked me up and down and said, "It's cool."

"What's cool?" I frowned, making a grunting noise.

"You've made yourself feel good in the skin you were given."

I was quiet for a minute. He was corny as hell, but I thought it was sweet. He could have just said, you a whole nigga, but instead he smiled at me and winked. I smiled back, knowing that he was trying to run a little game. He slid a hundred-dollar bill into my slot and one into his. The rest of the night was on and popping. He won a couple of thousand and I did, too. When it was all said and done, we retired to his room and slapped balls for the rest of the night. The rest is history.

"Bitch," I said to myself in the mirror, "we did not come here to play. We bout to get this paper."

Puncho came out of the bathroom as I squeezed into a tight pair of baby phat jeans.

"That ass getting thick." He said over his shoulder.

"Oh, hell no," I shook my head. "A couple of nights in the gym and a nigga will be A-okay."

"Yea, iight. Where you bout to head to anyway?"

"I got to stop by the office and chop it up with Bev about my trip to the island. I need her to hook me up with a couple of outfits and some money."

"Shit, I'ma bout to go see what's up with that nigga Fuzz. You know he want Sweets ass real bad. I don't know how much longer you could stall this shit."

"I don't either but trust me, I got you."

"He wants me to move some weight for him—from Brown's crib to the office. He said it's a couple thousand and some bricks. I need you to meet me at Brown's though."

"We pushing or nah?"

"Blind." He coded and walked out of the bedroom.

I tossed a black velour sweat suit and my bullet proof vest into a large duffle bag and grabbed my purse. Tossing the duffle into the truck, I snapped open the case that held two riffles. I made sure they were loaded and then hopped into my car.

When Shit Get Ugly

~Bev~

I was sitting behind my oak wood desk when Sandra switched into my office and placed her purse down. She crossed her legs at the knee and popped the bubble gum in her mouth. She was a little hood but classy. I knew when I first met her that I wanted her to be a part of the team. I was surprised, though, when Puncho agreed that she could work as a sexy decoy. He had been a part of our crew long enough to know that being a decoy meant fucking niggas you normally wouldn't. Sandra didn't seem to mind either, but she came with a price and a list of demands.

Whenever I sent her on a job, she requested a new wardrobe; a nice purse or a pair of shoes. She would get her weave reinstalled and her nails done. I didn't mind because together we have reeled in some big fish. She was my go to girl for getting shit done. Plus, she didn't need the training Drama paid for us to have. It was like she had been an assassin before.

"What's up, Mama?" Sandra leaned back and folded her arms.

"Same shit, just a different day. You know how the shit go." I told her as I typed something on my computer.

"Hell yeah. What's up with Drama?"

"Ain't talked to her in a while but I might go up there to visit, maybe take the kids."

"Have you talked to her about that? Bringing them up there?"

I rolled my eyes and shrugged. "What's the big deal? That is their Momma."

"You right but that's not the type of environment for kids. I'm just saying you should ask her about it before you take it upon yourself to take them."

"Anyway," I snapped, "what brings you here?"

"I came to rack up real quick. You know I got to be right for the trip."

"Yea, I know. So, you like him like that?" I chuckled.

Sandra nearly throw up in her mouth. "Hell no, you know this is strictly business."

"I hear you girl. Puncho will tear that ass up."

"You know it!" Sandra laughed.

I gave her the key to the dressing hall. There I kept hundreds of outfits and shoes for my girls. Some were used, and some were brand new. I watched her sashay out the office as Fuzz wheeled himself in. He greeted me with a big smile.

"Hey, baby."

"Hey," I responded dryly.

I still hadn't figured out his angle, but I knew that he wasn't telling me the whole truth. A part of me wanted to believe that he was down for me, but I could sense that he was on some other shit.

"Yo, what's really good?" He parked his wheel chair next to my desk.

"I don't know, you tell me."

"I can't tell you shit. You been acting like I did something to you or some shit. I always ride with you. Fuck with you cuz I love you but now you tryna switch the game up on me and shit."

"You moving like a whole snake. I ain't Drama. I love my sis but she was a youngin in the game and a lot of niggas took advantage of that."

"So, you comparing me to that nigga, Marquis?" he scrunched his eyebrows. "I ain't nothing like that nigga. I'm that same nigga that bailed your fucking ass out on them larceny charges, the same mother fucker that held shit down when you had to do a bid. And I introduced you to your sister."

"I appreciate all that shit, Fuzz. But what the fuck was you out here doing when I was laying up in the hospital with Aaron?"

"I was getting the paper, like I always do. I bring that shit back to you. I don't understand how you could ever doubt my loyalty to you when I'm the one riding around in this bullshit ass wheelchair."

"I put you there?" I rolled my eyes. "Ain't nobody tell your ass to go out there acting like you Superman. We got niggas for that. You said you was laying off all this shit, to focus on the legal part of our business. But I get a call," I mimicked a phone with my hands, "you done got shot up."

"Yo, niggas hit our spot. Tried to stick us for all our paper. It's my job to protect what's ours."

"You right, but like I told you before, no one even hit our shit." I shook my head.

"So, why the fuck these niggas still walking around?" He looked over his shoulder, referring to Sandra and Puncho.

"Cuz. I got to get the plan in order."

Fuzz snapped his teeth, "Bullshit! You ain't never take this long to pop you shit before... what's up?"

Fuzz knew that I was a hot head. I had been arrested several times for an array of charges, assault with a deadly weapon included. My heart didn't pump koolade and I was always strapped. I was waiting on the truth to reveal itself because I refused to believe that Sandra and Puncho came on their own. This was some type of Karma. Murda and Marquis were on the same team and I wouldn't be surprised if a decade of shit wasn't coming to haunt Drama and me. At the end of the day, I didn't know who I could trust.

The man that I loved was out here keeping secrets so there was no telling who else was. I stared at Fuzz while he sat across from me, in the wheelchair and prayed that he wasn't trying to see me fall either.

~Puncho~

I parked the car half way down the block from Brown's. Sandra rolled on a pair of black gloves and I pulled the ski mask over my face. The sun was just starting to set over the raggedy ass townhouses while I pushed up the back window of his apartment. We could hear laughter coming from a room on the other side of the house. I held a pistol to my side and Sandra pushed into the bedroom.

"What the fuck!" Brown screeched tossing the PS4 controller.

"It's the fucking boogie ghost." I snarled, pointing the gun at his head. He put his hand in the air. "Where's the fucking money?"

"I don't know what you talking about." He shook like a leaf.

"Where the fuck is the money?" Sandra yanked his head back and stared him in the eyes. "Tell us, we save you."

"Fuck no. ain't no money."

"So, I see you wanna do this shit the hard way!" she snatched the gaming system out of the wall and smashed it on the floor.

Brown yelled out in agony as he watched the small parts fall on the floor. "Okay," he mumbled. "The shit is in the safe."

I handed Sandra the gun while I reached for the safe. "What's the fucking combination?" I asked.

"2-8-1." He told me. "Look, don't hurt me." He cried.

I chuckled and popped open the safe. I dumped all of the money and coke into the bag. Then I went through the house searching for the rest of the shit I knew he kept there. As I walked around, I heard a sniff pop. Sandra emerged from the room and nodded at me. She grabbed the duffle bag and climbed back out of the window. Now, it was time for me to perform.

I pulled off the mask, stuffing it into my pocket. I walked out of the back door of the townhouse and around to the front. I pulled out my phone and dialed Brown's number.

"Ayo," I said to the little niggas, sitting on the porch a couple of houses down. "Y'all seen Brown?"

"Nah, ain't seen him all day." They shook their heads.

"That's strange," said an old lady, "it's after three. He usually goes to play the number."

"Really? He ain't been answering my phone calls all day." I started to dial the number again, pressing my head to the door. "I hear the phone ringing."

"His car parked over there." She pointed.

"Alright. Well if you hear from him tell him I came by."

"And what's your name sweetheart?" the old lady smiled.

"G." I told her and walked off.

A few hours later my phone was ringing off the hook. Sandra was on the bed counting the money we stole from Fuzz's safe. I answered the phone and tried to sound surprised when Fuzz told me they'd found Brown dead in his apartment.

"Man, shit crazy. I went over there. He wasn't answering the phone. Thought that nigga was sleep or something."

Sandra was rolling her eyes and making little faces. I chuckled lightly.

"What's so funny?" Fuzz asked on the phone.

"Nah, laughing at some shit on TV. I'ma come by there in a few and shit. Got to count the loses."

"Right, my nigga. Be easy." Fuzz hung up.

Sandra burst into laughter. "You feel good about my handy work, huh?"

"Hell yea." I kissed her on the lips.

It didn't bother me that she was born a man. I knew that I was attracted to boys since I was about ten. However, I wasn't the type to be walking around in dresses and shit. I was a thug, born into this shit. My father was the type of nigga to shoot first and never ask questions. He would run up on your Momma and your wife if you owed him money. He taught me never to wear my emotions. I didn't give a fuck about nobody at all. I started slinging rocks when I was eight—hustling in my building. My momma was strung out on heroine and didn't give two fucks if I was coming or going. Shit was different back then for a nigga like me. I was hustling to feed my two little sisters. When I got older, I knew that there would never be shit else out there for me. I wasn't some rich nigga who owned corner stores and nails salons. I was a regular, money getting nigga. I came from humbled beginnings and at one point, I was dead broke.

Fuzz put me on the game and I started to come up but not enough. I was trying to rule over the entire jungle. When I met Sandra and we came up with this plan I vowed that I would never eat Ramen noodles again.

Fishy Business

~Drama~

"Damn, Bev." I waited impatiently on the phone. "Answer."

Then, it clicked, and she said, "Hello."

"Yo... where you at?" I asked her.

"Home, why?"

"Yo, that bitch Sandra is a fraud."

There was a silence on the phone. I knew that my sister trusted her like she would me, but I had to let her know what I found out at the Chow. Sandra's ass was not at all who she said she was. We needed to get that bitch out of our camp and fast.

"What you talking bout, sis?"

"She's a man."

More silence. "Come the fuck on, we ain't got all day on the phone. I was at the Chow and some bitches was talking about a tranny from Midtown. They said that she was a straight savage. She was the one who killed Javy back in the day; bullet straight to the head. She went after big names and robbed them for everything they had."

"But that's why we hired her, right? To go after the big names."

"Yea, but she works for self. We the hook, Bev. You gotta get that bitch out."

"Man, this is way too much."

"No, it's not. Kill that bitch before she kill you." I told her and then, the phone clicked off.

"Fuck!" I slammed it down and went back to my cell.

I laid down on the bottom bunk and pulled out the book I had been reading. It had been six months since I been on the inside and there was nothing better to do in here then read. I mean the majority of the population was separated by cliques. I ain't really with all that shit, anyway.

"What you doing?" My celly came into the room and leaned on the frame of the bed.

"Same shit, different hour." I snapped. "Tryna get the fuck up out of here."

"On a murder? Girl, please. They fixing to chew yo ass up and spit you the fuck out." She said.

Julie was a tall butch bitch with big ass titties. She wore her hair in braids straight to the back. I ain't going to lie, I was scared of her ass when I first got here. she look like the type to eat a bitch pussy while she slept. Now, I have warmed up to her a little bit.

Besides putting a couple of dollars on my books, mother fuckers I thought had my back ain't got no love for me. How the hell did I end up here? I thought about all of the shit I went through trying to seek revenge on Murda's ass. Now, I was lying in this cell while the people who helped me are living it up on the outside. Life was a harsh son of a bitch.

~Bev~

So, my inclinations were right. Puncho's ass was on the down low. He was out there sucking dick and shit. I was wondering all of this time why Sandra's voice was so annoying. Now, I could laugh about the shit.

My girl was miles across the country and every part of me wanted to call her about the shit Drama told me on the phone. Upon meeting me, Sandra did say she was from Mid-town, but she failed to mention that she was a killer, specifically that she was the woman who killed Javy.

Javy was murdered on the roof of a hotel, slain and beaten to death. His face was so smashed in that he could not be positively identified by facial recognition. His dick was also cut off. The case remains unsolved. I can't say for sure that I believe that Sandra is the one who killed him though.

I mean there are a lot of rumors going on around the jail, like stories of the men Drama had taken to the bathroom. She would never be the one to set the record straight either so how did she find it befitting to relay a message to me about Sandra?

There was some bullshit going on in this business of drugs and death. I was going to get to the bottom of it though and you better believe I am going to come out on top. There were few things a mother fucker could fuck with, my man, my son, or my money. I wasn't too shy about blowing a nigga's head off right where he stood.

I hopped out of the bed and went to check on Aaron. He was snug in his crib. I smiled down at my sweet boy, glad that he was finally home with us. The rest of the house was quiet, Fuzz was probably in the den. So, I went into the kitchen and started to cook breakfast.

Although his dick could get hard, Fuzz and I haven't had sex. It wasn't that I wasn't horny, I just was afraid that he wouldn't be able to satisfy me. We would only be able to do it in one position any way. I need a variety. Hell, I am sure the shit probably fucked with his head too. He would get up early in the morning and go into the den. It wasn't just the fact that he couldn't fuck me how I wanted to be fucked but that I didn't trust him the way I once had.

Everything was different between the two of us since Aaron was born and he got shot. I tried to act as if it didn't bother me, but it did. I wanted to talk to him, but he always pulled the guilt trip. I would be devastated if our love ended the way that Marquis's and Drama's had.

My sister had to kill the man she loved because he was snake. That had to be the most painful thing she had ever been through. I can't imagine having to put Fuzz six feet under, but I would. I tried not to think about it and to have faith in my man, but it was hard. I wasn't raised to trust men. We been through too much for all of this shit though and I expected him not to hide anything from me. I was always down for him but now it seems like he only looking out for self.

I have a son to think about now and I cannot let this game take me away from him. I needed to know what everyone was up to; what their angles were. The first move I needed to make was to find out who Sandra is really riding for.

I thought she was a big sister to me, but she was keeping a fatal secret, one that could cost all of us our lives. If any of the men she fucked with found out that she was a man, they could potentially shred all of us to pieces. In the end, I wasn't worried about the war, but I didn't want her to die before I was finished using her. She was a good asset; literally and figuratively.

I wouldn't be mad if she just told the truth, but the jury was still out.

Fuzz

Sitting in the den, I knew that I needed to tell my wife what was up. She deserved the truth. But I also knew that she ran her mouth too much. I hated deceiving her. She has always been there for me. When that chick took me for my money. She found that bitch and made sure that she would never take another breath in her life. I wanted to grab her and spin her around and bury my dick deep inside her from the back, man I was craving that. But I knew I had to make sure these snakes would think that I was an invalid. And doing that and having her with that far off look in her eyes, would let them know that I was hitting it from the back. She always looked stupid for a few days after I tied that ass up and rammed it from the back. Just thinking about it. Made me hard as a rock. I missed her standing up with her leg cocked to the side while her ass waved up from me pounding it. I missed her damn near crumble to the floor from the orgasm I was giving her. Man let me cut this shit out. I couldn't tell her just yet. I needed to catch that snake ass Puncho and that dude in a dress Sandra out there. And Bev was so hung up on Sandra that she wouldn't believe that they were snakes.

Bev

I made a call to someone and we agreed to meet up later to discuss this Sandra situation. Just as I was about to call Fuzz to come eat, a call came in. It was a blast from the past.

"Hey what's up J!"

"Hey girl, how is everything?"

"Man, not so good. I got a trader in my midst."

"Funny that you say that, because I was calling you about that. You know Brown's death was not an outside job. It was an inside job, and this is going to cut deep."

"Who was it?"

"It was Puncho and Sandra!"

"Wait what!?"

"Well people didn't know that Brown's house was wired. He told me, so after everything was done. I pulled the tapes and looked them over. I saw Sandra and Puncho enter his house and remove all the drugs and money. Sandra was the one that killed him. Not only that, Sandra used to be a man."

"D just called me and told me the same thing."

"I am the one that told her. You know I got the inside scoop on all the jail talk. Sandra used to be called Teddy. He did time in here with me. When my informant showed me the before and after photo's, I sent a kite to D."

"Damn that bitch had me thinking it was Fuzz trying to betray me."

"Nope it is not him. They have been betraying Fuzz for years. He don't even know. That whole shoot out was set up by both of them. Sandra was the one that shot Fuzz in the back. Sandra is Murda's cousin."

"Get the fuck out of here!"

"Yes, and she is the one that wrote the letter that got Drama locked up."

"Oh, really now. Let me go and talk to Fuzz about this. Can you come here with the tapes?"

"Yeah I am on my way!"

I hung up the phone and tried to stop the room from spinning.

Just then Fuzz came rolling in the room. He noticed that I was about to faint and came over to me to steady me.

I'ma Get This Money

~Sandra~

"If it ain't about the money, don't hit my shit! Now, leave a mother fucking message at the beep!" I listened to the messages on my phone, noting that one number had called and hung up twice. Bev left me a message too. She sounded a little hasty on the phone, like she had an attitude. I was taking good care of her so what kind of gripe does her ass have with me? I am not worried, I'm in Jamaica having a blast.

Sweets was walking around the room ass naked, pulling on a blunt. It was that real shit, straight out the ground. Then, he sat on the edge of the bed and typed something on the phone.

"What you tryna get into?"

"Shit lay in this fucking bed."

"Oh," he put the blunt in the ashtray.

I smacked my teeth and picked up my phone. I was missing my man. I wanted to be at home with him, but I had to make the paper. There was no way I wasn't leaving this mother fucker with more paper than what I came with.

"Get dressed," Sweets ordered. "You been in this fucking room all the while."

"Who the fuck you talking to?" I raised my voice, forgetting that I was supposed to be the submissive side chick.

"You girl." he hopped up and pulled open the closet.

I got up and started to get dressed. I made sure I put the small pocket device I needed in my purse. This nigga got me fucked up. I thought, following him out of the room.

We stepped into the hotel bar where the room was crawling with all sorts of people. I laid my brown eyes on a skinny white woman, carrying a Louis Vuitton purse. That bitch got money. I sat down next to her at the bar and struck up a meaningless conversation. The bitch was acting like she didn't want to talk, I didn't really care. I pulled out my card scanner and attached it to my phone identity theft device and continued to order a drink as I swiped all of her credit card information. Stupid white bitch. The device scanned the area and I was able to swipe a few more cards before Sweets asked me if I wanted to go shopping. Of course, I did.

We were tearing the strip up but most of the time he was on the phone, talking so fast I could barely understand. He was setting up a meeting for a buyer. He wanted to expand his Mid-Town territory. Since Javy was killed there were a few blocks open. Hell, I thought as he continued to talk, them blocks belong to me. I was the…

"Hey, girl," he wrapped his arms around my waist and kissed me on the cheek. "I can't wait to fuck you. That pussy is so good."

That pussy is so fake.

"I can't wait to suck you, baby." I replied, seductively.

I was trying to pretend that his breath didn't smell like shit and that his hands were as rough as sand paper. I had to keep my cool. As soon as we got back to the room, I ordered Puncho some suits from Armani and paid my car note for a couple of months with some of the credit cards I had swiped. I moved some of their money into my accounts too. Bitch, I am a mother fucking hustler; ask about me.

My phone beeped on the nightstand while Sweets was sucking on my hand-crafted pussy. I reached over and answered it.

"Yerdie?"

"What up, Mama? Is the sun kissing my baby?"

"Hell, yeah." I tried not to moan into the phone.

"I just needed to hear your voice. Holla at you later." Puncho hung up, sensing that I was in the middle of something.

Sweets came up for air and kissed me on the belly button. I was getting ready to ride his dick like a porn star to convince him to take me with him to meet the supplier. I needed to get the scoop on their business. He needed to trust that I was just a piece of pussy and not working with the enemy.

"Damn, baby." He mumbled, laying down next to me.

"Baby," I kissed him, rolling over on top of him.

His eyes were still closed, and his hands were up over his head. A part of me wanted to shoot him between the eyes but I didn't bring a gun. Fuck it, I leaned down and kissed his full pink lips. I tried to imagine that he was Puncho. That made it easier to stand the smell of his breath. It was a mixture of my salty juices and the weed he was smoking earlier. Trying not to gag, I kissed over his hairy chest and my lips wrapped around his dick. I rolled my tongue around it and then took his balls into my mouth too. I sucked and licked on them really good before sitting up and planting my pussy on him. I was riding that dick like it was going to fall off and when I got tired I laid down next to him. He was smiling but his eyes were still closed.

He fell asleep and I took it as the opportunity to swipe all of the information off the burner phone he had brought on the trip. There were a bunch of outgoing and incoming calls to a specific number as well as some text messages. They detailed the drop and where he would be meeting the supplier. This was even better than him taking me with him. I texted Puncho and eased out of the bed and into the bathroom. I called him.

"What's up, baby?" he asked.

"Tonight, is the night. You got the flight info?" I asked him.

"Yea, I'm straight." He told me.

"Alright." I hung up the phone and started to get ready.

First, I braided my weave into a crown and took a shower. When I was done Sweets was already gone to meet the supplier. I slipped into a black sweat suit and pair of Nike boots. My bare face was still that of a man. I put on a pair of shades and slipped out of the room. Instead of taking the guest elevator, I took the service elevator down to the garage. I popped the locks of a Mercedes and hopped in, tossing my duffle bag into the passenger seat. I turned on the radio and some Beyonce song was playing. Riding out, I used a portable GPS to direct me to the place where Sweets was meeting the supplier.

It was a dark secluded area on the water. The moonlight lit the waves and I could see three silhouettes in the distance. Sweets was waving his hands back and forward, excitedly, with a big smile on his face. The deal must have been going in his favor. I tried to get closer, but I didn't want to risk being seen. So, I dipped behind a boat and tried to hear some of their conversation.

One of men tugged a large barrel onto the dock and Sweets pulled out a suit case.

"Pure," he said, sniffing a nail of white powder. "Load it," he said, starting to walk away.

Still ducked between the ships, I pulled a riffle from the duffle bag and aimed it at Sweets. I pulled the trigger, but the bullet split a sail instead.

"Fuck!" I snapped aloud and fired again.

Sweets was on high alert, pulling a gun from his waist band. He fired in my direction and then, bullets started flying from every direction. I didn't see sweets or the men who were with him. So, I eased from between the two boats and tiptoed to where they were. A few bodies were slumped over in various areas on the dock, but I still didn't see Sweets. The money had blown from the suitcase and was all over the place. I pushed the barrow of drugs on to the ship. The ship wasn't set to take sail until the next day, so I wanted to ensure that it would end up in New York, that's where Puncho would pick it up from.

My eyes darted around, and I still didn't see Sweets. I started to stuff some of the money into the duffle bag when I heard a loud bang. I looked up to see him shooting down at me, so I shot him off the platform he was standing on and his limp body fell into the sea. I continued to collect the money and got the fuck out of dodge.

I got back into the hotel room and turned on the TV. I laid there for several hours, trying to make sure all of my T's where crossed and all the I's were dotted. It was show time. The clock struck 3 AM and I called down to the front desk.

"Hi, um… I'm in Room 312 and my boyfriend hasn't come in yet. I was wondering if you could see if he is in the show room?"

"Sure, I will check for Mr. Fugi."

"Thank you." I said and waited.

She came back to the phone a few minutes later and informed me that he wasn't there.

"If I see him, Ma'am, I will let him know that you are looking for him."

"Thank you." I smirked and hung up the phone.

The time seemed to be ticking by slowly, but the sun slowly started to rise. I got out of the bed and worked myself into a frenzy. There was a message on my phone from the shoot out the night before. I ran down to the receptionist desk, screaming at the top of my lungs.

"He must be dead! My boyfriend must be dead!" I cried.

"What?" the woman was puzzled. "Calm down."

"He's dead," I replayed the message.

Every eye in the place was on me as I cried and screamed. Once I was calmed down and ushered back to my room, the police showed up. I didn't have any information, expect for the recording. They left, and I packed, the money too, to go back to the states.

Down to Ride to the Very End

~Puncho~

"Yo she lucky, I love her." I shook my head and closed the trunk of the rental car.

Then I eased up on the dock and waited for the ship loaded with Sweets' packages to sail ashore. A short skinny Jamaican man hopped off the boat and approached me since I was carrying a sign that said, 'Goodie Bar.' It was the code used in all of Sweets' drops. He nodded hungrily with a big smile.

"The junk is there." He gestured toward the ship.

I peeled a few bills from the roll of hundred dollar bills I had pulled out of my pocket and handed it to him. He smiled more and walked away.

Popping open the top of one of the barrels, I knew that Sandra had finally struck gold. We had done a lot of scheming in the time that we'd been together, but this was enough weight to help us move out the two-bedroom apartment we stayed in. I was ready to start a new life and leave all this shit behind.

I wouldn't say that I was flat broke when I started fucking with Fuzz, but I wasn't where I wanted to be. I was a regular nigga, hustling in front of the liquor store across the street from my Momma house. Hell, I remember days when I couldn't afford shit to eat but Raman noodles. I was getting by though. Randomly, I was talking to Fuzz at the bar one night and one thing led to another. He was the type of nigga a lot of other niggas envied. He had a couple of dollars and some whips to show for it. He and his chick were trying to make a name for themselves. I wanted in.

I waved in the direction of the driver in a white truck. Standing over to the side I watched them haul the barrows of dope on to the truck. Then, we rolled out of there as if nothing had happened. I hopped back on a flight and waited low until Sandra was to come home.

~Sandra~

The news was blazing with the story of a couple of village boys being found dead on the dock. One of them being my supposed boyfriend. When the cops came to ask about it, I cried and had a fit like any ole lady would do. They let me go home to the states.

As soon as I touched down, I went to the office to tell Bev what supposedly happened. She was pissed off that she didn't have the chance to catch the lick, but she was glad that he was gone. I wanted to brag about my shooting skills, but I knew it wasn't the time.

I sat back and listened to the stories of how Drama use to run this shit. I laughed at how naïve they all were when it came down to the game. They saw a bunch of dollar signs and designer backs. I couldn't believe she was actually walking up to random ass bitches on the streets and offering them a lavish lifestyle. She was young, though, and thought that every threat had weight. You see how that shit turned out?

"Damn, Sandra," Bev huffed from behind her death. "They found his headless body in the river?"

"They say a gator got em." I shrugged my shoulders.

She laughed. "That's fucked up. I sure wish I could have taken that ass to the cleaners though. Welp, one less thing for me to worry about."

I tooted my lips up, trying to bite my tongue. She was so stupid, so blinded. As I was getting up to leave, Fuzz rolled into the room. That man was the grimiest nigga I knew. He thought that his shit didn't stink. It did.

"Hey, Sandra. What's up baby girl?" he asked.

I leaned down on and kissed him on the cheek. "I was just asking Bev about you."

"Oh really?" he smiled in her direction. "What she say?"

"She said the dick was good." I reached to squeeze him, looking over my shoulder at Bev.

She lowered her head. From what I've heard though, he been giving her the shitty end of the stick. Fuck, I crack myself up. Let me get the fuck out of this office. I have money to count.

I couldn't wait to see my man. He was waiting for me in the middle of our queen-sized bed. I kicked off my shoes and slipped off my dress. My titty popped out and I swayed over to the bed. He was counting some of the money, but it was his suck that I wanted to suck. I leaned down on the bed and eased it from between his legs. It puckered up at my touch. My lips kissed around the head and then, I dipped my tongue into the deep tip and Puncho hissed a bit. The sound reminded me of the first night we made love. My hands caressed his legs and then, I slithered in between them. He was still counting the money while my head bobbed up and down on his big juicy dick. It was one of the better sized ones I have had. I guess that's another reason I opted to get a pussy. My asshole was starting to wear thin. Hell, these bitches out here with they pussies falling out; imagine how my asshole felt. Don't trip, I let him slide up in there every once in a while.

"Yo," I said, coming up for air. "What that lick read?"

"Your head game always been on point."

I mushed him, "I'm talkin bout the money, Stupid."

He laughed. "Damn baby. I miss you too." he reached for a kiss, but I turned my head. "Oh, so you acting stink."

"Nah, I gave you some head already. I'ma need to know what the money looking like, now."

"It's looking like 200K. I flipped that shit real quick. No need in getting our hands or noses dirty. We got to move fast and watch this shit bubble over. I want the fucking crown and these niggas gonna know my name."

That tough shit turned me on. I watched his nose flare up, wondering what the fuck made Puncho so mad. He scooted to the edge of the bed and stood up.

"That nigga had the nerve to call my fucking phone and ask me to go down to the Towers to collect. Fuck I look like? He better get one of his little runners to do that shit. I ain't that nigga puppy."

"Look," I interjected. "You need to calm yo ass down and go do what you got to do."

"Fuck out of here." Puncho snapped. "That nigga can suck my dick. You out of here…Tonight."

"And where the fuck are we going?" I asked, batting my lashes.

"Cancun." He stood up and left the room.

I leaned back on the bed and stared at all of the money. Puncho was putting on his big boy drawls and I liked that shit. I got dressed and started to pack the money. I was down to ride with my nigga til the wheels fell the fuck off. I just had to let go of any good feelings I had for Bev. This wasn't going to end well and that was a reality.

~Bev~

Something was not right. I could feel it. My intuition was telling me that I needed to stop something before it happened. I checked my watch and then, my messages. There were no clues as to what was happening, but I didn't feel safe. I picked up the phone and dialed the pager I had given my nanny. I told her it was a code blue. She need to get my son out of there and quick. I grabbed my purse and started to walk out of the office. Hearing the squeak of a pair of tennis shows, I spun around on my heels, vanishing my weapon from my purse. I fired two shots in the direction from which the sound came. Then, a few shots were fired at me. I dodged into a small crease in the wall and fired down the hall.

"Who the fuck is that? Come out here and face me, you fucking coward."

"Your mother is a coward, bitch!" A man shouted back.

The voice didn't sound familiar, but it didn't matter. They had the nerve to bring their ass on my property. The only way they would leave is through the bathroom. I stepped into the dimly let hallway and headed toward them. I walked up on the assailant and fired my weapon. They dropped to the ground and I pulled the mask off.

"Who sent you?" I asked.

"Sweets bitch!" he coughed up blood.

"Well he should have told your ass to come correct." I shot him in between the eyes.

The man was dead and still shooting orders? Something was a little fishy about all of this. I quickly dialed G's number and told him to come clean up. As I got into my car, I called Fuzz. He would have been the one I called on to rescue me in a situation like this, but that nigga can't walk.

"Baby calm down." He said on the other end of the phone.

"A nigga out here trying to kill me and you talking about calm down? Nigga, what?" I shook my head. "Look some shit going to go down and I need to you make sure you take care of Aaron."

"What?" Fuzz snapped on the other end of the phone. "My son always going to be good but you ain't bout to be out here moving all crazy. Bring your ass home so we can talk about this."

"Talk? I don't wanna talk. I'm sick of talking. Niggas need to know who the real don dada is around here. They out here thinking I'm weak and shit cuz Drama ass locked down. I ain't that bitch though. I ain't with all this negotiating shit. Someone going to give me the answers I want and now."

"Iight, I hear that hot shit you talking. You don't wanna listen no more. You must think cuz I'm fucked up, I won't fuck you up. Now, get yo ass home. Now!" he shouted and hung up the phone in my ear.

I tossed my celly in the passenger seat and sped off toward my house. Fuzz was in the living room, feeding the baby. I scooped him up and started pacing the floor. I could feel my blood pressure rising and my head was spinning in circles. Someone had put a hit out on my life. I won't rest until I find out who it was.

I guess mother fuckers were mad because I swooped in and took this game by storm. My people were moving weight in all five boroughs and some of New Jersey and Pennsylvania. I rarely got my hands dirty unless I was counting money. There were a couple of cats that probably had a vendetta against me. That was cool but to violate me by sending a mother fucker into my house to kill me was on a different level. Fuzz ass sitting here telling me to calm down. *Nigga, you calm down.*

"Now, you know we done pissed a lot of mother fuckers off in the last few months, especially since we created the signature blend. You have to be patient baby girl. The snake will come out of its skin."

He was really starting to sound like one of them. I side eyed him as I put Aaron in the bassinette. I sat down on the couch and took a deep breath. There were so many different scenarios running through my head, but one thing stuck out to me.

"Sandra," I mumbled.

"What about her?" Fuzz asked.

I sat up and turned to look at him. "Drama told me she used to be a nigga. She is a trained assassin."

"What?" He was shocked, and he laughed. "That can't be true. I done saw my nigga Puncho beat the breaks off some pussy."

"Damn, must be the only pussy he is getting cuz issa man!"

"Nah, can't be. Where Drama get this from?" his eyebrows were raised on his forehead.

"Some chicks in the chow," I shrugged my shoulders.

"Imma ask my nigga. Ayo, you know that nigga Brown's funeral is tonight."

"Oh really?" I nodded. "We have to go pay our respects, huh?"

"That was the homie. It's only right." Fuzz rolled out of the room.

I pulled out my phone and texted Sandra to ask if she and Puncho were coming to the funeral. I only half assed believed that Sandra was behind all of this. I trusted her with my darkest secrets and I know that she wouldn't betray me like this. But I also believe that Drama wouldn't have told me about her if she didn't think that something was amidst. My gut was telling me, though, that I have to get her to tell me the truth. Is she the one behind the hit on my head?

After calling a sitter for Aaron, I came down stairs in a black form fitting dress with a small clutch under my arm. It was big enough to fit a .22 in it, though. Fuzz was dressed in a black suit and a pair of fresh gators. Even handicapped, my nigga was fine and fly. My panties got a little moist thinking about sucking his dick and then, G walked into the room.

"What's up Princess?" He asked, hugging me.

"Nothing," I quickly pulled away.

"So, y'all ready to roll?" Fuzz asked.

"When you are, Boss."

G opened the door and I followed Fuzz down the ramp to the car. G helped him into the car and I took my seat in the front. G's cologne was lighting up the car as a brisk breeze flowed through the cracked windows. A sweet melody played while we pulled into the parking lot of the funeral home. It was crowded with people—friends, family, and crackheads alike. Brown's mother and father were greeting people at the door.

She pulled me into a snug hug and whispered, "My son was so grateful to you. We have to find his killer."

I smiled politely but the tone of her voice alerted me that she felt I was responsible for her son's death. I thought about the incident that had taken place earlier that day. Brown's family was now on the list of suspects.

They weren't the mafia, but his family had been known to slice a few niggas up and toss them in the Hudson. It was possible that they were on the hunt for revenge. I couldn't blame them, either. If someone had come into our home and shot Aaron point blank in the face, I would want their heads delivered to me on a platter.

Since the murder had been receiving some media publicity, I wasn't surprise that there were a few officers scattered in the crowd. They tried to blend in, but I could smell a mark from a mile away. They kept whispering and nodding. I sat down in the third row with my legs crossed. My eyes were fixated on the preacher and the choir.

It had always bugged me how a drug dealer or a killer could die and the whole family would swear he was a good dude. Brown was pushing weight on his block. In fact, he was ranked as our top dealer seven months in a row. Everyone knew that he was short tempered but here they were, at his funeral, praising the ground he walked on.

G tapped me on the shoulder when the service was over. "Yea," I looked at him over the rim of my shades.

"We bout to roll to beat the traffic." He stood up. "I got somewhere to be anyway."

"Like where?" I cut my eyes at him and he rolled them beady ass eyes. "Never mind," I mumbled, pushing Fuzz toward the exit.

When we were in the car, G turned on some Jazz music and I turned on my phone to check my messages. Drama had called to tell me she had some news and Sandra called to say she wanted to have lunch.

Since when did she want to have lunch with me? I frowned. I mean, I am always down for some good ass food, but Sandra and I have never been that tight. Sure, she had swooped in as a big sister to the game, but we were that type of friends. I contemplated meeting up with her as G pulled in front of our house. He opened my door before he went to get Fuzz's chair out of the trunk.

I couldn't wait to take my bra off. My titties felt like two boulders. I hadn't nursed Aaron in a few hours and them things were killing me. I unsnapped my bra as soon as my feet crossed the threshold and sighed a sigh of relief.

Jo-Jo, the baby sitter, was sitting on the couch watching some sappy Lifetime movie when I walked in.

"Hello," she greeted with a smile. "Aaron is down for a nap. He's such a good baby."

"Aww, aren't you sweet?" I pulled a hundred-dollar bill out of my clutch and handed it to her.

She stood and asked, "Is there anything else you'd be needing?"

"No, thank you." I told her.

I peeked at my sleeping baby and then, disappeared upstairs. It was time to unwind and possibly try to fuck Fuzz. It had been months since we'd attempted to make love and I was over do. I probably would have fucked G because I was so desperate.

I shook my head at the smell of his cologne or the tone of his voice. That man had the pour to make me feel uber sexy without ever even touching me. I touched my nipples and started to rub them when I heard a creak in the door.

"Don't stop." Fuzz smiled at me. "I think it's sexy."

I turned to him with a smile and continued to rub my nipples. I was doing it in a slow circular motion when suddenly milk started to squirt out of them.

Fuzz burst into laughter as I dived for a towel. I was screaming hysterically, "It's not funny! Stop laughing."

"Aww, baby, calm down." He was still laughing as I tried to make it stop. "It's natural."

"I cannot wait til it's over." I plopped down on the bed.

Fuzz rolled over to me and pushed my legs apart with his hands. I was embarrassed but it seemed to melt away when he kissed the top of my breast. Taking my nipple in to his mouth, he started to rub my clit. I moaned aloud while my hot box was getting wetter. Then, my body was spread out on the bed and my feet were perched on the arms of the seat while he dug into my soul with his tongue. He licked and slurped me as if I was his last meal. Stars danced above my head as I called out for Jesus, Buddha, and Allah. My hands gripped the cover and I could hear his tongue meeting my flesh. He bit my pussy gently and then, shoved two fingers into my asshole.

"Please," I begged, grinding on his hand and mouth.

"This my pussy?" he asked, in between licks.

"Yes," I yelled out, arching my back. "All of it!"

He pushed his face back into my pelvis and his fingers dug deeper into my ass. I was moaning so loud, I could have sworn I heard Aaron crying. By then, the bed and my face was wet with breastmilk but I didn't give a damn. Fuzz was making my pussy squirt.

"Traciiieeeee! Oh….Oh….Oh my god, I'm about to cum." I murmured.

"Come for daddy." He instructed, sucking my pussy.

"Yes. Yes…Yessssssss!" I screeched; a creamy white substance splashed his face.

He backed up and I hopped off the bed. Pulling down his pants, I positioned myself on his lap. My ass cheeks were slapping his thighs as I bounced up and down. Fuzz smacked my ass and called me, "Bitch!"

"Mother fucker!" I yelled. "This dick….this dick is so…."

"Yes, bitch! You nasty lil slut, fuck daddy dick." He smacked my ass again. "This your dick."

I leaned forward and used the bed as a brace as I threw it back on my man. I was waiting so long for that dick that it didn't matter that he had a shit bag. I didn't give to fucks that he was paralyzed, either. In that moment, he was the nigga I met when I was fifteen. I closed my eyes and remember the first time he and I fucked. It was nothing short of scary as hell but by round three, the little freak in me was wide awake.

Fuzz wasn't the only man I had been with since then but paralyzed and all, he would be the only man to ever make me squirt. I was so busy reminiscing, I didn't realize that I had come a few times.

Fuzz huffed behind me and patted my butt. I stood and walked into the bathroom.

"Your ass shaking like jello and shit," he giggled.

"Best you ever had!" I closed the bathroom door.

I pulled out my phone and sat on the toilet. Scrolling through MyBook, I couldn't help but laugh at the thirst of bitches. They put all their business out there and then wonder why a mother fucker talking about them. I have a page, but I don't post much. I use it to keep tabs on other mother fuckers. I mean, if I needed to stomp a hoe or shoot one, MyBook would let me know exactly where they were. Social media is all fun and games until someone get killed.

Ping. An instant message popped up on my screen. Intrigued, I opened it.

Mimi: Hey, I was scrolling through your profile and I think you're sexy.

Me: Fuck off bitch!

Mimi: You ain't got to be so mean! It's cool. I fucked your man anyway.

Me: Man.....listen lil girl. you best gone on head.

Mimi: Ask Fuzz how this pussy taste.

I hopped off the toilet so fast you would have thought my ass was on fire. Fuzz was lying in bed, flicking through the channels.

"Who the fuck is Mimi?" I asked.

Fuzz frowned until I shoved the phone in his face. "I don't know that bitch."

"Man, she knows you." I snapped. "Who is she?"

"Girl," he waved his hand. "I ain't got no time for this shit."

"Let me find out you fucking some bitch! Im'ma shoot you and this bitch!"

"You wilding. When the fuck do I have time to fuck some bitch? Last year, maybe but recently nah."

I mushed him. "The fuck you mean, 'last year'..."

"Just what the fuck I said."

Oh, this nigga tryna act like he don't know me, I thought. I folded my arms across my chest. "Who the fuck you been fucking?"

"You wanna know? You really wanna know?"

"Man fuck you!" I shook my head and grabbed my pillow. "I'm sleeping in Aaron room." I stormed out.

I prayed that he was just saying things to get under my skin and I hoped that Mimi's ass was playing tricks. I laid down on the twin sized bed and checked my phone again. There were no more messages from Mimi and for a moment, I wanted to go back to my own bed. My neck was hurting but I had to let Fuzz's ass know that I wasn't going to tolerate him doing whatever he wanted to do.

I was always willing to be his down ass bitch. I would take a bullet for that man and bust a cap in a bitch ass for him too. It wasn't always roses and butterflies for me and him. For the most part, I trusted him, but Momma always told me that if they cheat once they'd do it again. I love Fuzz, but I will kill his ass dead and he knows it.

Just then my phone rang, it was J.

"Hey sorry I couldn't make it the other day. But I'm outside right now."

"Come on in."

I yelled upstairs for Fuzz.

"I'm coming he said."

J sat at the table and started pulling out her laptop and all the evidence she had.

Fuzz sat there watching and wondering what the hell he was looking at. There was nothing for me to say. Drama was looking out even from the jail.

Fuzz finally spoke. "Them motherfuckers is dead!"

"Naw, not just yet. Let's just chill and set them up. I have a plan for them." I smirked.

"Hmm that look, I have seen it before. When Drama set them bitches up." J said.

"Yeah they do have the same facial expressions." Fuzz laughed.

"Now fill us in." J said.

"Well Sandra and Puncho hit him in Jamaica and had the drugs shipped to them here. She doesn't know that I know the full story, she called me with some bs story about what happened. I got connects in Jamaica that had already told me the full story. As a matter of fact, they are scheduled to leave in the morning for Cancun. We can strike their spot and take it all. When they come back they will have nothing." I exclaimed laughing.

"And I will get this info over to my connect in the prescient. Including the forged note and the text messages between Murda and he/she." J said.

"Good I will call the boys and have them clean them out in the morning." Fuzz said.

"Them backstabbing bitches is going down. And once they hit the jail, I will take it from there. You know I got people on both side of the jails. I will put the word out that he like fucking dudes. And that she is a dude by nature." J said.

"Good I will see yall later."

"Thanks J have a good night."

"I can't believe that he is pitching for the other team." Fuzz laughed.

"You just found out your boy set this whole thing up and all you think about is he is pitching for the other team."

"Yeah man because he thinks he got the upper hand on me." Fuzz growled as he stood up from the chair.

I snapped my neck so hard with my chest pounding. "You been playing me all this time?"

"Well..."

"That's why that dick still get hard when I walk by." I laughed.

"I couldn't tell you. You would have given it away. I set the whole thing up with my doctor. I was wearing a vest that night. He knew better than to call me for shit like that. So, I knew it was a set up. I have been on P for months. Someone in the camp told me he approached them to come at me. But see when you feed your people right, you ain't got nothing to worry about. I'm sorry I had to keep this from you, but common sense should have told, niggas don't get hard when they are paralyzed." He laughed.

"That shit is not funny. I was about to kill for betraying me."

"Well now you can fuck the shit out me." He said picking me up and carrying me back to the bedroom.

That night we did it four times before I passed out. I now know what my husband was hiding from me and now I could put my trust back into him.

My nipples were beginning to hurt, and it woke me up. I got out the bed and went to check on Aaron. He was up and reaching towards me.

"Good morning baby boy, you ready to eat?" I said lifting him out the crib and holding him tight.

He latched on as soon as I put his mouth there. I was singing to him when Fuzz walked in the room.

"I am glad to see that he is sleeping through the night now." He said kissing me on the forehead.

"Yeah me too. He is a good baby." I smiled down at him.

Fuzz bent down and kissed him on his forehead, "you look just like your mama. I'm going to take a shower and call the boys."

"Ok babe."

I switched Aaron to the other nipple and rocked gently while he played with my face. When he was done, I burped him and gave him a bath. I woke up the other kids and waited for D's morning call while I cooked breakfast.

D called after they ate, and I asked her if I could bring them to see her. She told me no, so I left it alone. I didn't want to tell her about everything that I found out. I didn't want to get her hopes up. I knew with Jodi on the case she would get her out. And I know that she would be out by the months end. But I was told to be quiet, so I was going to be.

I got the kids cleaned and ready for school. I got Aaron dressed and waited for the nanny to pick him up. I needed to go to the office and get some work out on the street. I knew that when the boys brought the stuff from Puncho's, I would need to divide it up and get it out ASAP. Fuzz was going to stay home today and work from home. Now that he was walking, I had to act like he was still crippled. When the nanny came we, all headed out the door. I dropped the kids off and headed to the office. Sandra and Puncho's flight left when I pulled into the parking lot, according to the text that Fuzz sent me.

~Fuzz~

I waited at home to hear from Mark about the apartment. I was still reeling from hearing that Bev was about to kill me. I wasn't surprised though; my Queen was not one for the disrespect. Even though I played the field before and she knew that I had kids, I stopped all of that when we got married. But I also know that I have to get rid of all those dating sites I was on. Whoever that chick was that hit me up almost got me merked.

Sucka Free

Sandra

Flashing back to the first time we tried to hit them. Memories flooded my mind....

It was rare that I was fearful. Most of the time I was prepared to do and say whatever I wanted. Like the time, I stepped out of my bedroom wearing my mother's dress and high heels. I looked that woman in her face and said, "I was supposed to be a girl." She was pissed off for a while but, eventually, she got over it. When Teddy became Sandra the fear I once had, had all but died.

I was going to conquer the world—the underworld especially. My first priority was to kill Javy. He was the one enemy I could never let go and it gave me great pleasure to put six rounds into his ass. Since then, I had murdered about twenty niggas. I was proud of that but today, I was staring in the mirror, unsure of if I was going to return home that night.

Fuck, I snapped my teeth, looking down at my Iphone. There was a message from Puncho but I wasn't ready to answer. He keeps telling me that I need to hurry up and get the shit done and over with but I'm stalling.

Hell, I ain't even sure why. I have never feared a bitch who blood look like mine. Why the fuck is this shit taking me so long to do? I looked at the phone again and turned it face down. I was trying to get my mind right.

I walked into the bathroom and turned on the tub. Pouring a lot of bubble bath into the water, I started to undress. There was a blunt on the edge of the sink, waiting for me too. I lit it and sat on the edge of the tub. I inhaled deeply and realized that time was not going to wait for me. I stepped into the tub and continued to puff on my blunt. I reached down and began to stroke my pole. I wanted to make sure that I was relaxed. After I busted, I knew I needed to get rid of this thing if I was to become a full woman. And to accomplish that. I needed to get out and hit Javy now.

"How the fuck did I get here?" I asked aloud.

Once upon a time, I was living in a condo on South Beach. My father was born in Jamaica and had worked on a farm that grew marijuana. It was his job to pluck it and grind it down. The farm owners packaged it and sold it at the market. One day, my father met a man named JR.

JR was the head honcho of one of the biggest drug trades in Jamaica. Nothing moved in or out without his say. He paid off politicians and police to make sure that his army was secure. He ordered my father to grow extra weed on the land without the owner's knowledge. He'd then sell it to JR. That was my father's big break. Later, he became a runner for JR. He met my mother a few years later in California. I was born and Papi continued to run for JR. When I was sixteen my father was savagely murdered.

I later found out that his demise was because of an affair he had with Beverly's mother. JR was devastated that his mistress was sleeping with another man, let alone a mere farmer who worked for him. So, he beheaded my father and tossed his body in the river for the alligators to eat.

At first, I didn't care to ever meet Bev or Drama. Their existence was of no interest to me. I was getting my own money. I was the Sean Jean of South Beach. Whatever kind of drug you were on, I had—coke, heroine, roxies, mollies, mary jane, percs, and the list goes on; hell, I even sold mushrooms. My name rung a bunch of bells, especially in Javy's ear. He asked me to come to New York so that we could strike an exchange. I was down to make whatever money there was to be made. I was starting my transition by then.

When I came to New York, I was still a burly dude, but I wore a weave and a push up bra. This pissed Javy off. He cursed me out and put me out of his club. He said that no fag would ever shake his hand. I was fine with that until he started to blackball me.

It was about revenge from that point on. After kidnapping his bitch, I ordered my entourage from Cali to come and off ten of his street hustlers. Three long ass weeks of unrest in New York City, there were news cast and protesters everywhere. They were shouting to save the streets and me and my hitters were there, marching with them. I was even interviewed for the papers.

Then, I got whiff that JR's daughters ran a turf on the other side of town. It was the sweetest set-up. I sent a few threats in Javy's name. They were furious, so Bev sent her niggas to murder a few of Javy's. It was on like popcorn. I shot Javy point blank and joined Bev's team.

Now, I'm lying in this hot as bubble bath, thinking about how I am going to kill Bev. I wish there was a better way to do it, you know, like send her off to be happy somewhere but I knew that was too farfetched. She had to go. I needed a quick come up so that I could get this money to disappear.

~Puncho~

Where the fuck she at? Why she ain't answering the phone? We got moves to make if this shit fixing to go right. I ain't got time to be playing all these fucking games. I dialed the number back and still, no answer.

It had been eight years since I been in so deep. I hadn't caught a real lick in the game since I popped a nigga named Chris. That was my come up. I took that nigga for everything he had; his drugs, house, car, and his bitch. I was banging that bitch back out so much that she spit out two of my seeds. Then, the broad decided that this wasn't the life for her and moved down south somewhere. I ain't seen my kids since. Some nights I lay awake and think about that shit, then, I look at Sandra. How can I raise my kids knowing I'm sleeping with another man? Perhaps they're better off without me.

Drugs have always been an easy way out, either I was selling them or doing them. Being a product of a crack head, I knew first hand that this shit could ruin lives, but I didn't give a fuck. I was so hot blooded, that I was ready to blow a fucking gasket. All this waiting shit was really pissing me off.

Sandra and I have the weight we need to start off fresh. We could roll out now and leave all this shit behind. All I want her to do is see this shit my way.

"Man fuck this shit," I revved the engine of my car and sped off.

Pac was blazing in the speakers as I sped down the road toward our crib. Sandra had better be sleep or some shit. I was starting to think she was regretting shit, but we are already in too deep. I had killed about five niggas in the past month. So, I was ready to get the big fish.

Fuzz and I went way back but that shit was true what they say, 'if it don't make dollars it don't make sense.' He was getting in the way of my money and I couldn't have that shit. True, dude had put me up on game back in the day but now I was a grown ass man. All the deals we made and the connects he set up, I could easily stand on my own. Besides half the time I was meeting with them anyway. So why the fuck did I need him.

I pulled up to the crib and hopped out of the truck. Music was playing from the bedroom and weed was in the air. I stepped into the room and saw steam coming from the bathroom. I was still pissed the fuck off. I couldn't believe that all that money we stole was gone. Now we had to move to get this shit back. We had to do it. It was no longer a want but a need.

"Yo," I pushed open the door. "Why the fuck you ain't answering the phone?"

Sandra sat up in the tub and rolled her eyes. "Damn, baby, you scared the fuck out of me."

"Nah, you scared me." I sat on the edge of the tub and grabbed the rag.

She leaned back in the tub and I started to wash her. "What's up with you shorty?"

Sandra shrugged her shoulders. "I don't know baby."

"You are having second thoughts?"

"We need this bread. I got to do what I got to do, right?"

"Yea, but you know you can talk to me."

She smiled and said, "I know baby and that's why I love you." She reached for a kiss.

"I love you too. Man, the fuck up and let's roll on these mother fuckers."

"Man up?" she tried not to laugh.

"You shot the fuck out cuz you know what I mean."

"I guess you right. I'm still a nigga at heart." She stood up, water rolling down her nearly six-foot figure.

I stepped out of the bathroom and sat on the edge of the bed. I pulled out my gat and reloaded in the chamber while she walked around the room, naked.

"You know, I really fucks with you." She nodded. "You get to see me like this—all vulnerable and shit.

"Yea, and vice versa. You know I got cha back baby."

"True, daddy." She took a deep breath and then, sat on the bed next to me.

"Relax, baby."

"Imma try. Supposed to go out with Bev tonight. You know she been asking why I been distant. I got to keep a straight face. My trigger finger be happy as hell when I see her, though."

I shook my head and stood up from the bed, picking up a blunt from the ashtray on our nightstand. I lit it and took a long pull. Smoke rings circled my head as I opened the closet door. We had five shoe boxes filled with cash and jewelry we stolen. Plus, a box of credit cards and IDs. I pushed the clothes aside and pulled out an AK47 and a few hand guns. Sandra was on her side of the closet getting dressed.

"You ready to roll?" I asked over my shoulder.

"Let's do this shit, already." She grabbed one of the guns and led the way out of the house.

This what made me fall for her ass in the first place. She was about the shit. She might tense up at times but when her mind was made up, it was time to shoot first and ask questions later.

She didn't give a fuck about shit and her tunnel vision was on as we hopped in the truck. She was loading the guns while I sped off toward one of Fuzz's spots. He called me earlier in the day and told me he was going to kick it and play cards with a couple of his hittas.

His car was parked outside of the joint as we cased it. "It's about ten niggas in there and two bitches. We got to do the shit fast." I told Sandra as I turned the corner down the block.

When we passed the second time, Fuzz was standing outside on the porch. Sandra eased the window down and sprayed the house. Caps were busting back at us.

"Fucckkkkkkk!" she screeched as I pulled off.

"You good, baby?"

"Fuckkkkk. I got hit!" she screamed.

Damn it! The tires screeched as I slammed into a alley. She was doubled over, and blood was squirting out everywhere. I turned on the light and tried to figure out where it was coming from. Tears were streaming down her face. I hopped out of the truck. Her side of the car was riddled with bullet holes.

"Hold on baby, I got you." I let the seat back and ripped open her shirt.

"Did I hit that nigga?" she asked through clenched teeth.

"Baby, I'm only worried 'bout you." I told her as I found the whole. "Fuck!" I snapped my teeth.

"What? I'ma die?" she quizzed.

I ran and popped the trunk. There was a first aid kit and some thread. I had to get that blood to stop. I wasn't a doctor, but I learned some shit out here in these streets. I grabbed everything and started to clean the wound on her shoulder. It looked like it was a flesh wound so I sewed it the best I could. She was screaming and hollering but it was what it was. I hopped back in the truck and drove to a parking lot. We switched cars and I hurried up home.

After getting her comfortable on the couch, I gave her a few pain killers, so she could go to sleep. My phone was ringing off the hook. It was one of the little niggas calling to tell me that the spot was hit. I told them I was going to meet them at the building.

When I got there, Bev was sitting in her chair with a disgusted look on her face. I looked around and Fuzz was sitting there too. The room was quiet, and all eyes were on me.

"What the fuck happened?" I asked.

"You tell me…" Fuzz shook his head.

"I don't know. Jason called and said…"

"The spot got hit." Bev finished my sentence. "Where's Sandra?" she eyes me.

"Why? She got to be at every meeting now or some shit?" I snapped.

"Pipe your fucking voice when you talking to my wife you buster ass nigga." Fuzz stood up.

"That was your truck, wasn't it?"

I shook my head. "I don't know what you talking about my nigga."

"My nigga?" Fuzz laughed. "We ain't been niggas in a long time. See, I know a lot about you."

"The fuck you think you know about me, Money?"

Fuzz walked around the table and got all in my face. I looked the nigga square in the eye and said, "What you know, nigga?"

"You's a two-faced ass dog. You been playing this shit the whole time. You got beef with me, you punk ass nigga, why you ain't been killed me? You got your bitch out her riding harder than you."

82

"Fuck you, nigga." I pulled out my gat.

I pointed it at Bev and suddenly I was surrounded by niggas with guns.

"This between you and me, my nigga." Fuzz mocked.

"You right, you pussy ass nigga." I pointed it at his head.

"I dare you." He laughed.

He hit me in the arm and the gun fell to the ground. Then, he and the other niggas wailed on me; beating my ass until I fell on the ground. They picked me up and dragged me into the dungeon under the building. Fuzz tied me to the chair and slapped me across the face with a pistol.

"Bitch ass nigga! You ain't talking all that shit now!"

I spat blood at him. "You a weak as nigga, kid."

"Man, shut the fuck up. You swallow kids every night. Gay ass fucking with a nigga." He laughed.

Then, everything went black...

Free: Almost

~Drama~

"That's that straight fuck shit I was trying to tell sis about." I paced back and forth in the little ass cell. "I know she is going through the shit."

"Calm down. There ain't nothing you can do about that shit from in here," my roomie tried to tell me.

I wasn't trying to hear it though. I wanted to punch a hole in the wall, but it was concrete. Bev sent me a kite and it wasn't looking pretty on the outside. I wished that I was there to help my sister out of the jam, but she was capable of doing it on her own. So, I sat down on the edge of the flat mattress and put my hands over my face. It was stressful as hell not being able to be there when the one who needed me was out there hurting. "Drama!" One of the inmates ran up to the cell. "What's good Scoob?" She asked with excitement.

I cracked a little smile at her enthusiasm. She was a chick I knew from the block. She was thick and black; reminded me of a baby ape. But she was quick with the hands so at times I had called her to smack a couple of little bitches for me. Last year she got bagged for possession of a firearm and a robbery. Now, she was in here doing a 5 to 10. The shit was crazy but hey, everybody got to eat.

"What's good my nigga?" I slapped hands with her.

She laughed and said, "You out here sounding like a whole nigga in these streets."

"Nah, never that. I still like my cinnamon." I told her as we slapped hands. "What's going on, Yonda?"

"Ain't shit. Yo, my celly talking some straight bullshit. Talking 'bout she got an escape plan."

I shook my head and listened to her tell me the plan. For a minute, the shit was sounding alright. I mean, these weak ass CO's would do just about anything for a lick. Pop name still rings bells out in the street so hell, I was liable to make the shit work.

I leaned back on the bunk and stroked my chin. My mind was in a million and one places but the best place was home. I missed my son. I would have done anything to hug and kiss on my baby one time.

"Damn, Yonda, that shit might just work though." I looked at her conspicuously. "I heard that these CO's ain't worth shit in here. I bet if we slung them some pussy, we'd be able to get the fuck out with the quickness."

"Bitch!!!!" Yonda exclaimed. "You crazy as hell. I ain't bout to get caught out there like that."

"Why the fuck not? You wanna go home, too, right?"

"Not that fucking bad, sis." She rolled her eyes.

"You ain't got to front for me. I know yo ass home sick and shit."

Yonda looked away. Shit, I'm in this bitch worried about my family every day and I would give a nigga my soul if it meant I could go home.

I thought about the night I got bagged. Bev and I were on our way to the city. It had been a while since I had gone out. Truth be told, I was still mourning the fact that the man I loved never really loved me.

I thought back to that day....

"Damn, chile," Bev said from the passenger seat, "Slow the hell down. The city ain't going nowhere."

"My bad." I turned down the music. "I don't realize how fast I drive sometimes."

She laughed and shook her head.

Typically, I was fearless. I never thought twice after leaving the Bathroom. I didn't care about the consequences of my actions nor who would be hurt in the end. But as I stared at my son in the rearview mirror, I was remorseful. The hardest thing I would ever have to do is to explain to him that my hands had killed his father. I knew that he might resent me or even hate me for half of the things I had done but I was out for revenge. In the end, it was worth it. I found out Marquise's true colors. So, I hoped that our son would understand that I killed him for the both of us.

As I cruised down the road, an uneasy feeling came over me. I wanted to vomit but I closed my eyes and took a deep breath; looking over at Bev. She was mouthing the words of a song that was on the radio and rubbing her protruding belly. I smiled, knowing that she would be a great mom soon.

"Damn, girl," I said, exiting the parkway, "you going to burst any day now."

"Please don't say that. I ain't ready."

"I know, she need more time to grow."

"She? Why y'all swear it's a she?"

I was about to reply when an officer flashed his lights behind us. Bev looked at me and I looked back at JR. My heart was pounding relentlessly in my chest and I was starting to sweat. I took a deep breath and pulled into the shoulder of the road. The officer got out of the car and tapped on the window. I rolled it down and batted my eyes at him.

"How may I help you, sir?"

"Ma'am, I've ran your license plate and this car has been reported stolen. Please step out of the vehicle."

"What?" I looked over at Bev.

"Put your hands on the stirring wheel and down move." He told her, raising the gun.

Grace bit her bottom lip. "Officer, my son is in the backseat," she explained. "Can we do this nicely?"

"Ma'am, step out of the car." he opened the door, "and put your hands on the hood." He pulled me out of the car and started to pat me down. "Grace Lee, you are under arrest for the murder of Marquis Anderson. Anything you say can and will..."

"What?" Bev hopped out of the car. "What's happening? Where are you taking her?" she asked.

"Ma'am get back in the car," he pointed his gun at her.

I cried, "Please, Bev, just get in the car. Take him home."

At that moment my life went from sugar to shit. I was hauled off to the precinct where they interrogated me for hours. They had even threatened to have me deported. I wasn't talking though. There was no way I was going to give them an ounce of hope.

Thinking back, I was shitting bricks—scared as hell that I might end up like Sandra Bland. I wasn't ready to die, I had too much to live for, but I wasn't going to spend the rest of my life in jail. Here I am, though, pacing back and forth in this fucking cell. Shit, I'm mad as hell and that escape plan sounds real good. I miss my son and all my family.

"Yonda," I looked at the girl. "Tell your celly to meet me on the court later."

"Are you serious?" she frowned.

"Like a mother fucker," I smirked.

Yonda left the block and I laid back on the bunk. I stared up, thinking of how it might feel to fuck a CO. It had been almost a year since I had some good dick. My pussy was thumping at the thought of it. At that point it wouldn't have mattered who's dick it was. I remembered a time when I was scared as hell to give up the pussy, now I was willing to sell it to get the fuck out of here.

Hell, I wasn't supposed to be here in the first place. My 23-year-old ass was supposed to be in college somewhere; getting the finer things out of life. But this drug game chose me. That shit chewed me up and spit me the fuck out. I was wondering about the life I could have had if I had listened to my father. I touched my neck where the necklace he gave me use to be and closed my eyes. I knew he was probably flipping over in his grave. I was the son he never had though. I had to give myself props, I was running shit solo when I was on the streets. I just fucked up on giving my heart away.

I had always wondered why a lot of the niggas in my circle didn't fall in love. Love was too fucking dangerous, and I learned that shit the hard way. I couldn't believe I was so fucking stupid. I could guarantee your ass one thing though; when I do get the fuck out of here, I will never let my heart talk for me.

Around six we all went down to the chow. They were serving some dogfood-looking shit but when you're starving, you get used to it. So, I sat at the table with my roomie and six other broads. We were laughing and talking about the good ole days. Laughter was the only thing that would keep you sane in here. I had to make a few friends and a couple of enemies before anyone would sit at the table and laugh with me.

I was used to being the outcast but in this prison, these bitches praised me. All the stories that emerged surrounding Marquis's death had brought me fame. They thought I was a bitch to be feared. At heart, I didn't feel like it though. I was weak. I was lonely and moreover, I was scared. I didn't want to spend all of my life here. I was too young and too pretty. When I looked in the mirror, I saw my father. Not the young vibrant version of him but the one who watched me leave the house that day. The man who had so many enemies that his own brother would fuck his wife and his best friend would kill him. He was worn out and tore up. I looked like that and worse every day that I spent in here.

"Yo," Yonda and a skinny chick sat down at my table. "This is my celly. Chelle, this Drama. She from BX."

"What up though?" I slapped her hand. "So, what you in for? You look like you're 'bout 20."

"22. I got caught transporting 100 keys."

"Damn." I shook my head and stuffed some broccoli in my mouth. "You know the trade, huh?"

"Something like that, you know they be trying give basketball numbers for these charges. But that shit neither here nor there. I just wanna get the fuck out of here and Yonda said you with the shit."

I shook my head and took another bite of my food. I looked at the girl over the rim of the milk carton. I eyed her from the face down. She was a pretty girl, but life had left its bumps and bruises. Shit, she could have been a part of my crew. I was intrigued by her confidence. She wasn't like many of the other girls. She gave off a different vibe.

"Yea, I'm with the shit but we got to have an iron clad plan. No talking, no fucking up." I told her.

Fuck Boy Blues

-Bev-

The phone rang at about 3 in the morning. I reached over and answered it.

"Ayo," a familiar voice said on the other end. "Come out side right quick."

"What's up?" I looked over my shoulder at Fuzz.

"I just need you to come outside right quick." He told me.

I eased out of the bed and tossed on my house coat and slippers. This nigga got a lot of balls, I thought as I went downstairs and opened the front door. He was parked in the driveway. I slid into the passenger's seat and he rolled off into the darkness.

"We can't keep doing this." I whispered.

He put his hand on my thigh and said, "You like this shit."

I blushed, knowing that what he said was true. Sneaking off into the night was thrilling. As much as I wanted to put an end to it, I knew that I wanted to let him fuck me until I couldn't breathe. He pulled up to a small house on the other side of town and we both hopped out of the car. As soon as the door was opened, he pulled me into his big black arms and wrapped his lips around mine. My pussy was soaked as he pressed me against the wall and rubbed my bare clit.

"You want me?" he asked me.

I moaned but didn't answer his question—my hands in his pants. They dropped to the floor and I was on my knees. His dick was long and thick. I wondered why it had taken this long for us to fuck. I was trying to play hard to get but he always had a thing for me. I took his dick into my mouth and sucked it tightly. He was moaning and groaning, his hand on the back of my head. I looked up at him while he bit his bottom lip. As he was about to cum, I stood up and leaned over the table in the foyer.

He eased his bare dick into my throbbing pussy and held on to my hips. I clutched the edge of the table and thrust into his waist. He was holding on tight as my fat ass cheeks slapped against him. That dick was so damn good, I was speaking in tongues.

"You need to leave that nigga."

"Would you just fuck me?" I snapped back.

When we were getting it, the last thing I wanted to talk about was some other nigga. All I came for was the dick—the conversation was unnecessary. He grabbed me by the hair wiith one hand and by the throat with the other. He shoved his dick in my pussy and set in with short deep stroke. I groaned, longing for more. His grip was tight around my neck and I could hardly breathe.

"This my pussy?" he asked. I grunted in response.

He, then, let me go and walked off toward the back of the house. When my legs decided to move, I followed him into the bed room. I sat on his lap, his dick sliding back into me.

"Damn," I bit my bottom lip and came on his dick.

He lifted his hips and banged into me a few times until he came inside of me. He kissed me on the lips and tapped my leg. I slid off of him and sat on the edge of the bed. His thick white cum was dripping down my leg and suddenly I felt ashamed.

"We can't do this anymore."

"So, after you swallow my seeds with your mouth and your pussy, you decide we can't do this anymore? Well, you should have thought about that shit before you got out of bed and hopped into my car. I'm sick of playing this fucking game with you, Bev. Either we going to keep fucking like this or I'ma have to kill that nigga."

"He supposed to be ya boy…"

"And you supposed to be his wife." G went into the bathroom, leaving me with my thoughts.

Fuck, I stood up and went into the bathroom in the hallway. His cum was sticking to my thighs and I smelled like sweat. I took off my night gown and hopped in the shower. I couldn't go back home smelling like I had just run a marathon. The water soothed me, and I wasn't thinking about G or his antics. This would be the last time we fucked behind my husband's back.

I was starting to think it was about more than the sex. He already knew everything about our business. I knew he had a hidden agenda. He was trying to set me up with all this good sex. I wasn't falling for the shit because I should have never fucked up in the first place.

I fucked up.

He was waiting for me in the car. we drove back to the house in silence. I looked at him over my shoulder as I got out of the car and then, slammed the door shut. When I got in the house, Fuzz was in the kitchen.

My heart sank. I probably looked like I had seen a ghost.

"Where the fuck you been, Beverly?"

"Uh…I… Cindy called me and…"

"Who the fuck is Cindy?" he frowned.

"The neighbor…" I pointed over my shoulder. "The neighbor, she called me and said that her dog had got out. We were out there looking for him."

Fuzz laughed and stepped toward me. I stepped back. "So, you mean to tell me, Cindy…the neighbor drives the same car as my best friend and y'all was out looking for a motherfucking dog at 3 in the morning? Do I look like I was born yesterday?" he barked, grabbing me but the throat.

I saw a rage in him that I hadn't seen in a long time. I wanted to try to run but my feet wouldn't move. He started to shake me, and I grabbed his hands.

"Please," I cried, trying to catch my breath. "Please, Fuzz."

"Bitch! I should kill you!" he screamed.

"I…" I started to screech when he let me go.

Fuzz stared at me as I laid on the floor. "You fucking that nigga?" he reached down and ripped my night gown. "You say that nigga name when you fucking him, huh?" he asked.

I shook my head. "You know…"

Fuzz grabbed my titty and squeezed it. Then, he bent down and rubbed my clit. I curled up, thinking, he's about to rape me. Instead, he laughed and said, "You silly ass bitch!"

I didn't say anything as he walked in circles around me. His voice was low, and I could hear the pain in it. All this time, I had been faithful to my husband. Down to ride with his ass at all cost. I knew about Sheri, Yaya, and Take but I never said shit about them hoes. I chucked that shit up to the game but here he was judging me. I laid on the floor and took a deep breath before springing to my feet.

"Yea," I grunted with base in my voice. "I fucked him. It was good too. He ate my pussy so good, it's still jumping. Wanna feel it?"

"You slick talking whore!" Fuzz screeched pulling his pistol from his boxers.

I threw my hands in the air. "So, what you going to do? Shoot me? Nigga I dare you. You ain't got that type of heart."

He wrapped his finger around the trigger. "You weak ass bitch," he said as he pointed it.

"Shoot me motherfucker! Shoot me right here!" I pointed at my chest.

Tears welled up in his eyes and a vein was poking out on his forehead. My heart was pounding in my chest and I was low-key scared as fuck. I had seen love kill before. There had been times when I questioned how much Fuzz really loved me, but I now knew that he loved me too much. Tears rolled down his cheek as he pointed the gun at me.

"Out of all the niggas out there… all the niggas out there, and you fuck my boy? My best fucking friend?"

"Baby…"

"Don't fucking baby me!" he waved the gun. "We got a fucking kid together and you out there fucking these other niggas."

"It was a mistake. I didn't mean to…"

"So, what? You slipped and fell on that nigga dick? How long you been fucking G?"

There was a deafening silence. "I said, 'how long have you been fucking that nigga?" I didn't say anything. "How long have you been fucking that nigga, Beverly?" Fuzz moved closer to me.

I backed up, but he grabbed me, pointing the gun to my head. His bottom lip was curled up under his teeth and sweat was rolling off his forehead and on to my cheek. I closed my eyes and thought about our sweet baby boy. There was no way I was going to let this nigga kill me.

I jerked my arm, elbowing him in the stomach, and then I stomped on his foot. Bending over in pain, he let me go and I ran upstairs to the bedroom to get Aaron. As I carried him out of the room, Fuzz was staggering up the stairs.

"Where you think you going? You ain't taking my son nowhere." He yelled.

"You need to get some sleep. We are going to stay somewhere else."

Fuzz laughed loudly and launched up the stairs. "Bitch! You ain't going nowhere with my fucking son. You stupid slut!" he reached for the baby and I pushed him out of the way.

He still had the gun in his hand. I reached the first step and he pulled me back by my robe. The butt of the gun came crashing down on my face. All I could do was hold on to the baby. Had I let go he would have rolled down the stairs. Fuzz beat me in the face with the gun while yelling and screaming that I was a whore. My son was screaming, blood splattering all over him.

"Please, Fuzz, get off of me. The baby…"

"Man…" he grunted, smashing my face again.

"Please!" I cried, turning my face from side to side.

Then, he stood up and went into the bedroom.

I tried to open my eyes, but they were swollen shut. I felt all over for the screaming baby. I didn't think he was hurt so I eased off the steps and felt my way down the hall to his room. Envisioning how it was set up, I placed Aaron in his bed. I was getting ready to sit down in the rocking chair when I heard a loud boom. Bloody tears dropped from my face and I screamed.

"Fuzz!"

The baby stopped screaming and my face was throbbing, but I reached over and pressed 1 on the house's speed dial.

"Hello?" G answered on the other end.

"I need you to get here fast." I told him through swollen lips.

"On my way."

G hung up the phone and I sat there praying that he could get there in time to help us. I rocked back in forth in the chair, listening to Aaron's breaths. It had been a long time since I had done that, and this felt surreal.

What the fuck had I done? I asked myself. I felt my face and looked at my hands with blurred vision. I was glad though that I was dead. I was almost certain that Fuzz was dead though. It was all my fault. I had killed the man that I loved.

"Bev?" G asked from the door frame. "Oh my God, Bev. Are you alright?"

"I don't know," I mumbled. "Check on Aaron. Is my baby okay?"

I could hear him shuffling the covers and then he said, "Yes, he's fine. Where's Fuzz?"

"In the bedroom." I told him.

The bedroom door creaked open. Suddenly there was a loud yelp. "Oh, my fucking God! Dawg, what the fuck did you do?"

~G~

I cradled my best friend in my lap. He and I had been tight since diapers. Fuck, I should have listened when Bev said that all of this was a bad idea. I let my dick do the talking though.

Fuzz had shot himself in the head. Blood was all over the bedroom and the gun was still in his hand. Tears were flowing through my eyes, but I had to call someone. I dialed 911 on my phone and waited for the ambulance to arrive. They took Bev and Aaron to the hospital and I followed behind in my car.

Her jaw was broken, and her ear drum had burst. She was shaking and crying. All I knew to do was to be there for her. So, I laid next to her on the bed, and held her tightly in my arms.

"Where's Aaron?" she squeezed my hand.

I put my hand on top of hers and whispered, "He's fine, okay?"

"How did I get here? I mean, one day everything was good and now, we are in the middle of this shit? I just want out."

I laid there for a minute, staring up at the ceiling. I wanted to offer her the world, but I wasn't about to be her rebound nigga. So, I didn't say anything. I let the medicine take her to sleep. When she was sound asleep, I eased out of the bed and put my jacket on.

"Damn," I said aloud, kissing her on the forehead. "I'm sorry, Ma."

I never meant for this shit to happen this way. I wanted to have Bev in the worst way, but Fuzz wasn't supposed to off himself. I mean, let's be real—that was some fuck nigga shit. He killed himself over a bitch. There are so many other bitches in the sea though. I shook my head as I left the hospital.

I cruised down the road, Future buzzing in my ear, then the phone buzzed on the seat, next to me. Sandra's name flashed on the dash board and I sucked my teeth as I picked up.

"Have you seen Puncho?" she asked in a sweet feminine voice.

"Fuck you mean? That nigga ain't in my pocket." I snapped.

There was a brief silence. "He ain't been home in a few days and I knew he said he was going to run a lick with Fuzz. He ain't answering his phone either."

"He ain't never going to be answering that shit again," I told her as a matter of fact.

"Huh?" She was shocked. "What you mean?"

"Sweetheart, the nigga is dead."

"Who? Puncho? Fuzz?"

"Fuzz. He gave his self a shot to the dome," I said, dryly.

More silence. I whipped my car into a parking space and asked, "So, if I see that nigga you looking for I will let him know." I hung up the phone.

I wasn't about to sit there and talk to that fucking he/she any longer. That shit was still blowing me. My mind drifted back to Bev. I was ready to take Mama away but a part of me knew that her heart was still in the game.

She and Drama were born into this shit. It was all that they knew. Having a real nigga like me on her hip might ruin her life. I was going to protect her, though. That nigga Sweets has some heat waiting on her ass. If she thought Fuzz fucked her up she had another thing coming from her.

I rolled a blunt, remembering the conversation I had overheard a few nights before. I was at the Katz lounge, you know, throwing dollars at the hoes, when I spotted this motherfucker named Quanny sitting at the end of the row.

Quanny was a scrawny little nigga who swore he could rap. I saw him in a few shows, but you know these New York niggas overdo it. Anyway, that nigga was sitting at the end of the row chopping it up with another cat named Mal. Mal was tall black and ugly. He slangs rocks down on 23rd. A lot of the cats out their say he got stain, claim he chopped a nigga up and mailed him to his mother. I half ass believed that story though.

I inched closer to where they were sitting because I knew both of them fucked with Sweets. Quanny told Mal that the next spot they was hitting was one of Bev's. He said that he knew Puncho and that would be his squeeze. Of course, I was amazed by the whole thing because I thought Puncho was down for the name.

Right then, the whole game became clear. Puncho and Sandra are both playing for the other team. If Bev isn't careful, we will be burying her next.

One Down

-Sandra-

I rolled from under the bed and damn near ran out of the master bedroom. I didn't want to see his blood splattered all over the room. I've killed before but, I had never been that close to being caught. Bev's ass almost got in the way.

I eased out of their back door and tiptoed down the drive way. There wasn't much activity around seeing as though a murder had just taken place there. I climbed into my car and drove to the building.

My gut was telling me that Puncho was dead, but I had an inkling of hope that my baby was still alive. He wouldn't leave me without a fight. Honestly, I was better off dead than he was. He was just a pawn. I was that one that Beverly really wanted.

I didn't blame her either because without me, she would have everything she ever wanted. Too bad there were two of us that wanted the top of the town. She was going to have to learn the hard way.

I used my finger print to gain access to the building and headed straight for the murder room. It was dark and cold. It felt as if I was walking into a mortuary. There was medical equipment scattered about and the room wrecked of blood.

In the distance, I heard faint whimpering and sniffling.

"Puncho?" I asked, flicking on the lights.

He sat up straight in the chair he was tied to and jerked his body. I grabbed a knife and set him free while snatching the cloth bag from his head.

"You don't know how happy I am to see you." I kissed the top of his bald head.

"Are you alright?" he asked me.

I nodded my head and kissed him again. "I'm fine, baby. Are you okay?"

"Yea," he winced in pain, "a couple of broken bones but I will be okay. We got to get out of here."

"You need to go to the hospital."

"And tell them what?" he looked at me, blood oozing down his forehead.

"You've been in a car accident."

I helped him out of the chair and into the car. He was whining and crying as I put the petal to the metal and drove as fast as I could. I whipped the car into a few circles and crashed into a pool.

When I woke up, the car was surrounded by police, fire fighters, and ambulance. Puncho wasn't in the car next to me and it was flipped upside down.

"Ma'am." I heard a man say. "Ma'am, can you hear me?"

I only nodded.

"I'm Allen," the man told me. "I'm going to help you out of here, okay?"

"Where's my fiancée?" I looked around.

"He's okay. We're going to get you out of here." He re assured me.

I tried to keep calm with the noise of machines drilling into the car around me. I felt like I was on an episode of Grey's Anatomy. What the hell have I done? All I wanted to do was make sure Puncho was alright.

It seemed like hours had passed before they finally got me from underneath the car. I was rushed to the hospital, but I couldn't feel my legs.

"Allen!" I screamed at the EMS worker. "I cannot feel my legs."

"You're okay, calm down!"

"You've been telling me to calm down all damn day. I cannot be calm. I can't feel my motherfucking legs, my nigga!" I barked at him.

The look on his face went from day to night when he heard my manly voice. I had forgotten in the moment that I was Sandra. I couldn't feel my legs and this jerk was telling me to calm down. They better hurry up and get me to this hospital before I snap his twiggy ass in two.

The ambulance came to a halt and the back doors flew open. They whisked me out of the back where doctors awaited. This was some real live TV shit and all I could think about was Puncho. There was no telling how long he had been down there or what they had done to him.

They cut my dress opened and started to access my wounds. After ordering a CAT scan and some other bullshit, the room was quiet except for the beep of the machines. Then, a policeman walked into the room. I rolled my eyes and held my breath.

"Sandra Cox?" he asked.

I nodded my head.

"Can I come in and ask you a few questions?"

"Sure."

"What happened tonight?"

"Well, I was driving up the ramp and suddenly something hopped out of the bushes. I tried to swerve around it but…"

"Take your time…"

Suddenly tears welled up in my eyes. "I just got to know if my fiancée is alright."

"I… I don't know but he was hurt pretty badly."

"Oh my God," I put my hands over my mouth.

A doctor walked into to the room, "Where's Sean? Sean Johnson…"

"He's in surgery. He suffered some significant injuries."

"Some of which didn't occur as the result of the car accident." The officer butted in. "Sean was shot."

"Shot?" I frowned. "I picked him up from a little joint over on 65th Street. He hopped in the car fast and told me to drive. I don't know what happened to him." I lied, tasting revenge as I spoke.

"Sir…"

"No. Address me as 'ma'am,'" I snarled.

"Ma'am, something happened before the crash and I know you know more. Just cooperate and we will make sure you're taken care of."

I frowned. "Look, I don't know what you're talking about so… Can you please leave?"

"I'll be back though. Here is my card." He placed it on the table.

"Sandra," the doctor turned to me when the officer left, "Your

leg is broken in three places. You will need surgery. I have scheduled it to be done first thing tomorrow morning."

"Will I be able to walk again?"

"There is a possibility that you may lose sensation in one or both legs. We won't know until after the surgery. However, I am confident that with physical therapy you will be fine." He smiled.

"Fuck!" I shouted in frustration.

I rested my head on the bed and closed my eyes for a second. I could hear voices coming from the hall. The medicine was starting to kick in and I felt drowsy.

Faintly I heard someone say, "I'm here to see Beverly Lee."

The voice was familiar, and I knew that they were referring to Bev.

"The officer told me she was on this floor."

One of my eyes popped open as I listened for the nurse to tell the strange woman where Bev was. She repeated the room number and I made a mental note. My legs were fucked up, but my fingers weren't. One of us ain't making it out of this mother fucker alive.

I will have all of the cash and everything else. I am the real Don Dada, whether it be male or female. I'm in this shit to win it. I done already took the shit too far and my boo upstairs in somebody operating room. Shit was going to get ugly before it got pretty and that's on my Momma.

Let's Blow This Joint

-Drama-

"Yo," Drama whispered to Yonda, "It's time to make that move."

Visitors were starting to pour into the chambers as the girls watched from a bench. Yonda stood up and pulled the fire alarm causing everyone to move into a frenzy. The guards were yelling and screaming while a loud speaker message ordered for everyone to evacuate. The three of them stripped from their prison attire to reveal citizens clothes underneath, escaping alongside the crowd of visitors.

Once they were outside of the prison walls, they hopped into an unmarked vehicle. Drama sighed and yelled, "Thank you so much for coming to the rescue."

"Nah, no problem, Momma." G pushed the pedal to the metal and they sped away.

Drama had no idea that her plan was going to work. She was still scared to death because now she was on the run. G dropped her and the two accomplices off at a hotel and handed her the bag of supplies she had asked him to bring. She presumed that her face would be all over the news, so she would have to disguise herself.

While in the bathroom of the room, she took a deep breath and said good bye to the baby doll look she once had. She cut her thick bushy hair into a bob and dyed it jet black. Then, Yonda helped her strap the pregnant belly to her body. Yonda and her cellmate were set to leave on a bus soon, so they changed their clothes and got ready to go.

Drama waddled to the bed, as she had done when she was pregnant with JR and picked up the phone.

"Hello," his sweet voice answered.

"Hey, baby." Drama said with a smile.

"Momma?" there was so much excitement in his voice made her heart melt.

"Yes, baby. It's me."

"Oh my God. I can't believe it! Is it really you?"

"Yes, and I'm coming to see you." I told him.

"I cannot believe it, Momma. I can't wait to see you." He responded.

I hung up the phone with my son and started to get dressed. There was a knock on the door. Who in the hell could it be? No one knew that I was here. I didn't say anything as I walked to the door and peeked through the peep hole. A woman was standing there dressed in a black dress with a big black hat. She knocked again and then looked directly into the hole.

"It's me, Grace." She whispered.

I opened the door and pulled my Momma into the room. She wrapped me in her arms and hugged me tightly. A tear spilled from my eye. I couldn't remember the last time I hugged my mother. It was the most surreal feeling because I didn't think I would ever hug my mother again. It reminded me of the hug she and I had when my father was killed. I never wanted to let her go.

I knew that she didn't want this life for me. If she could have chosen, she would have wanted me to be a lawyer or doctor. She wanted what was the best for me, but I was chosen for this. My father left the seed in me and there was nothing I could do about it. Here I am twenty-six and running from the law. I didn't know what my next move was going to be, but I knew that I would never be apart from my family again.

"Momma," I looked at her as we pulled away. "I'm sorry."

"Chile," she looked at me, "You don't have to apologize. You are your father's child and I never expected any of you to get off scot free. I want you to know, though, that I love you and I will always have your back."

"But I know this isn't what you wanted for me."

"No mother wants this for their child. It wouldn't have mattered if you were a male child. I would never have wanted this for you. I just have to ride with you, no matter the trial."

She sat on the bed. "But, tell me, what's next? You know they're going to be looking for you, especially since Fuzz is dead."

"Dead? Momma, what are you talking about?"

"He shot himself in the head."

What the hell? I sat down in a chair. Why would he commit suicide? Out of all the selfish things to do, he would take himself away from his wife and kid? Bev must be going through it. Tears were starting to pour from my face.

"But that's not all," she said. "Bev was hurt pretty badly, too. G told me that he is the reason behind all of this."

I frowned, not sure of what my mother was saying. She went on to tell me about the affair. I was shocked. I thought Bev and Fuzz had the picture-perfect marriage, now I was not sure. Damn.

"Where is she?"

"In the hospital with a broken jaw. The business is falling apart Drama. There is almost nothing left. They are taking everything." Momma couldn't hold it in any more. "I think they are going to repossess my house."

"What? Momma, please say you're joking."

"I wouldn't joke with you like this, Grace. Whoever is out for your sister is trying to get it all."

"Momma, have you heard from Sandra?"

"Who? That he-she?"

"Yea…"

"Sandra called me the other day and said that Bev wanted her to move some of the money."

Money? I shook my head and bolted to my feet. "When I find her ass, she is grass." I grabbed the track phone and called G.

I told him to find out where she and Puncho were. I was ready to boil their asses. I knew that she was behind all of this. It was all coming together. She was going to fucking die if it was the last fucking thing I did.

For all I fucking knew, Murder sent her ass to take his down. The work of the devil was never through. None of it matter though because I am back!

Vengeance is Mine

Shit was getting crazier by the minute. No one knew who was playing for what team. It seemed like the more I tried to own my crown and make sure shit ran right, the more problems we had. I am ready to be done with all this shit. What the hell am I fighting for? My daddy is dead. My man is dead and if I don't stop I might be dead too. I thought being hard was in my blood but if it means the life or my son, I might as well check out, how can I leave my son in this world as a parent-less child?

Mama helped me into the wheel chair and strolled me to Aarons room. It wasn't fair to him that he had spent so much time in the hospital. He deserves more than this. I have to be here for him whenever he needs me.

As I stroked the side of my son's face the door crept open and a woman walked in. She cleared her throat and asked, "Are you Beverly Fields?"

I scrunched my eyebrows, "Who are you?"

"I'm Shaniqua Watkins from the Child Protective Agency. You must be Mrs. Fields."

"I am and what's going on?" I frowned.

"I understand that an incident occurred at your home today. Your husband beat you and committed suicide. The baby was in the home at the time, correct?"

I lowered my head and closed my eyes. I could still hear the loud noise of the gun shot. Was there something else going on with my husband that I didn't know about? I tried to focus on the matter at hand but then, I broke down. Mama wrapped her arms around me and kissed my forehead.

"Let it out, baby." She told me. "Ma'am can this wait?"

"No this is an urgent matter concerning the welfare of this child. I need to ask Mrs. Field some questions." Shaniqua shook her head.

"I'm sorry. I don't know what part of come back later don't you understand but my child is grieving, and she needs some time alone with her son."

"I understand, ma'am, but what you need to understand that if a hair on that child's head is harmed, it's my job on the line."

Momma's eyes got wide with fury. "Who in the hell do you think you're talking to? I will drag your half-baked ass out of here."

I pulled away from my mother's embrace and looked up at the CPS worker. "Ms. Watkins, I will answer any questions you have."

"Now," she cleared her throat. "Aaron was in the house at the time of the incident and so were the other kids."

"Yes," I told her. "Tracey and I were arguing. He hit me, so I went upstairs to pack a bag for Aaron and the other kids. Then, Tracey grabbed me and beat me in the face with the gun. I had Aaron in my arms, shielding him. When Tracey let me go, I ran into the nursery and he went into the bedroom. I couldn't see but I made sure the baby was okay by touching him. That's when I heard the gun shot and then Gene came to help me." I told her.

"Has there been any history of domestic violence in the house?"

"No, ma'am."

"What did Mr. Fields do for a living? Do you work?"

I looked away, ashamed to tell her the truth. The truth may get my baby taken away from me. I thought about that and said, "He was a defense attorney. I haven't worked since I was pregnant with Aaron. He was born premature, so he needs me." I stroked my baby's hand, fearful that it may be the last time I saw him.

"Understood. Mrs. Fields, while this is still an ongoing investigation, your son will remain under your care with doctor's supervision. There will be set limitations though."

My mother was sitting in the corner, rolling her eyes. She was getting ready to curse the young girl out, but I knew that she was just doing her job.

"These limitations will include an armed guard being at Aaron's door at all times during his stay in the hospital. At the end of his time here, we will inform you of our decision of his custody."

"Custody?" Momma cut in, "Ain't nobody taking custody of my grandbaby. She is capable of taking care of him."

"There is speculation," Ms. Watkins looked at me, "that your daughter is a drug dealer."

My head was banging. Did I hear her ass right? The pigs are on to me? The fuck is happening right now?

"What?" Momma screeched. "My daughter is not a drug dealer. She is a college educated woman, has a degree in education, too."

I lowered my head and tried not to burst my Momma's bubble. She had sent me to college, but I didn't graduate, hell I didn't even make it to sophomore year before I was arrested. There was so much about me, about my life that my momma didn't know. I tried for so long to keep it that way. She would stand here and go to bat for me though because I am her baby girl.

"Mrs. Fields, please be prepared for all of the allegations they will have against you. There is a reason all of this occurred tonight and the NYP will get to the bottom of it, one way or another. This will not be the last time you see me," She stuffed our file into her briefcase and turned on her heels. "Take care."

Shit just got real. I closed my eyes and envisioned Fuzz laid out on the bed. How could he put me through all of this shit? I couldn't envision these mother fuckers taking my son. There was no way I was going to sit around and let that happen.

"I got something to tell you," Momma whispered.

I looked at her as if nothing would surprise me.

"Drama is home."

My jaw dropped. How in the hell did that happen? She was in jail for murder. Who is she snitching on? I leaned back in the chair but didn't say anything. Too much talking was going on, anyway. I was ready to kill me a motherfucker.

As Momma strolled me back to my room, I saw a stretcher in the hallway with a curly weave hanging from the top of it. It reminded me of the wigs Sandra wore. I frowned, with a nasty taste in my mouth.

"Yo, I need some more pain killers." I heard a rusty voice say and then, my heart was in the pit of my stomach. It was Sandra.

"Coming up," the nurse said sarcastically.

I grinned. We were all under one roof and shit was fixing to hit the fucking fan. When Momma got me back to the room, I called G and let him know that Sandra was here too. I told him to go check the basement where we'd left Puncho. My intuition was telling me that he wasn't there though. Sandra was a riding type of girl and there was no way she was going to let him rot in there.

All I could hear from the room and around me was the sound of beeping machines. Occasionally a few nurses would be talking, or a new trauma patient would be rushed into the ER. Then, the curtains pushed back, and G appeared in front of me. He had grown up from that little boy in high school he was the grown man who was fucking me three ways from Sunday. I was getting wet, thinking about that last nut. Reality set in, that juicy wet cum was the reason I was laid up, getting medicine pumped into my veins.

He smiled and sat down next to me on the bed. "You alright, in here?"

"Yea, I guess so. Did the bitch rescue him?"

"You already know. Means he got to be in here somewhere."

"Well, Momma told me they done put her in a room."

"Oh okay. Don't worry your pretty self 'bout about. I will take care of it."

I smirked, "If I had a dollar for every time a man said that…"

"There you go, comparing me to these other niggas. Have I ever let you down?"

I shook my head. "I think you have, once."

"Uh?"

"When you let Fuzz have me instead."

G gave me a salty look. "You are tripping."

"Not really. But that's neither here nor there. We cannot go back and right our wrongs. So, lets kick it right now. You and the crew going to clean this shit up, right?"

"For sure." He nodded.

G laid down in the bed next to me and kissed me on the forehead. I was trying not to worry about what Ms. Watkins had said but I was worried, especially after Momma told me that Drama was home.

-Drama-

I slipped the pair of shades onto my face and slithered out of the hotel's lobby. I moved quickly into the black town car that G had left me and drove to the hospital.

Beverly was lying in the bed, G's arms wrapped around her. It was a crazy sight to see because I hadn't imagined the two of them together. He looked like he was comfortable but with these niggas nowadays it was hard to tell whose love was genuine or not.

I cleared my throat and gently closed the door. Bev's head popped up and she smiled.

"Hey, Sis."

"Hey baby." I kissed her on the cheek.

She reached out and poked the baby bump I sported and laughed. "Bitch, you done put on some weight. But you know what it do?"

"Of course." I smiled and showed her the syringe in my purse.

"That's why I fucking love you." She smiled as I took a seat.

"Chile, I'm hot as fuck."

Bev laughed and wrote something down on a piece of paper. I read it and nodded my head. I suddenly felt like one of the detectives from the Mission Impossible movie. I shook my head and stuffed the note in my pocketbook.

Flashbacks of all the shit I had been through in the last year ran through my head. This was a legacy passed down to me from JR. I was sure that Drama was not going to fail me now. It always followed me, no matter how good I thought I was doing.

A sly grin was etched on my face as I stepped into Sandra's room. She looked to be in a lot of pain. That gave me pleasure. Nothing was better than seeing the enemy lying in anguish. I was 20 and cashing checks. I wanted to bring the best on to the team. I didn't understand that everything that looked good wasn't good for me. I slipped up and now I was back to claim my crown. I run these running streets.

Sandra must have been knocked out cold because she didn't hear me walk into the room. I eased to the side of her or him; whatever she wished to be. Her eyes popped open as she tried to focus on my face. She couldn't, and her eyes quickly closed back. "I will deal with you later." I scurried out of the room. Then, I went upstairs to find Puncho's room.

He was in worse condition than her. He had several surgeries and managed to survive what should have been a fatal crash, but he would die anyway. I left the room laughing.

Their lives would go down as murders, but they'd never know how or who. I left the hospital, running down the back staircase and out of an emergency door. I got back into the town car, speeding to the sound of Beanie Siegel. I rode past the pizza shop where I had met Marquis with a salty taste in my mouth. I wanted to vomit but I kept pushing toward the safe house. I couldn't stay at the hotel another night knowing that they would be hot on my ass. I closed my eyes when I finally parked the car.

Walking inside, Momma was waiting there with Jr. and the other kids. We ran to each other and hugged and cried. I missed my little people and Jr. was getting so big and he looked just like his dad. I cried even harder knowing that I was going to have to tell him the truth soon. Momma cooked dinner and the kids went to do their homework. I went upstairs to get comfortable and find what I needed. Locating the file, I called who I needed and got myself a pardon and also one for Bev. She needed to be home for Aaron. The escape was covered by time served. Jodi was next on my call list. I was glad they didn't find out that she was a part of the plan. But she knew that she needed to be out on these streets.

I walked down the stairs and kissed my mom, "It's all behind us. I took care of it."

"Hey baby what do you have for homework?" I asked Jr.

"Coloring and math!" He said excitedly.

"Wow do you need any help? Do any of you need any help?"

"No mama we can do it!"

"Ok babies, grandma and I are going into the next room to talk. If you anything, just call us."

"Ok mama. Mama where is dad?" He asked as tears welled in my eyes.

I sat down and put him on my lap. I knew that this day was coming but not this quick.

"Well Jr., daddy went to heaven. He was a bad person that tried to hurt the people that loved him. So, we had to send him to be with God." I said.

"I understand mommy. I am sad that he can't be here with us mommy," he cried.

"I am to baby. I miss him too. But you can always see and talk to him. You look just like him. Just look in the mirror and talk to him," I said.

"Ok mommy," he said getting up.

I wasn't sure that he understood, and I knew somewhere in the future, we would need to have this conversation again. I went to talk to mama and tell her about the call that I just made. I assured her that everyone was safe now. I would personally go find the money that that Sandra stole and let everyone know that Jr's daughters were back into the game. I knew that with the two of us, there was nothing that we couldn't accomplish. Now that I was out, things were going back to normal. Nothing was going to be the same. Only family would be involved, and when I say family. I meant Bev and me only. Everyone had to go.

"Grace, I want you out of this business, but I am also realistic and know that it won't happen. You are your father's daughter and so is Bev. But I suggest that you stick to family this time. No outsiders," she advised.

"Mom I would love to stick to family, but family will screw you faster than strangers will," I said.

"Not your cousin Jr. He has always worked in the shadows for you. I never let you know. But he has been watching your back for years. When you went away. He watched Bev's back. So, I guess it is time for you to put him in the light," Mom stated.

"Hmm so you have been watching my back?" I laughed asking a question.

"Of course, I am going to watch my babies back."

"I see," I said standing up hugging her. "Maybe you're right."

Jr. was my father's sister's son. He was a straight up savage. He worked for Parliament in Jamaica. When someone needed to be eliminated, they called on Jr. If you saw him coming at you, it was already too late. I always wondered where that shot came from when I got surrounded on that drug deal with Paco. All I heard was shots ringing out in the distance, and all I saw was Paco's men falling. I guess I know now who was behind it. Just as I was finishing my thought, the doorbell rang. It was Jr. He was so handsome. He looked just like my dad but with a blond mohawk. I never understood why Jamaicans wore those crazy hair colors. I was never a fan of it.

"Hey Jr.!" I said running giving him a hug.

"Hey D, so happy to see you. But this is not a social call. There is something at the house that I need you to see."

"Ok, let me grab my keys and we can go over."

"We need to scoop up Bev on the way. They are releasing her today."

"Ok."

We left and went to pick up Bev. She was all ready to leave and G was there with her.
"G, I need you to take Aaron to my moms at the safe house. We need to make a quick stop," I said.

"You who is this?" He said looking at Jr.

"This is our cousin Jr. He is cool." I said.

"What a gwan big man!" Jr said, shaking his hand.

"Hey my nigga." G said shaking it back. "Ok, I will take him to your mom."

"Thank you, I am sure we won't be long" Bev said.

We all left, and G headed to see my mom. We headed to the old house. When we pulled up, Bev started crying. I grabbed her and helped her out the house.

"Fuzz is dead because I cheated on him!" She cried out.

"No, he is not. You don't know what happened. But Jr. is about to tell us both." I said.

For Jr. to be here, I know he found something.

We opened the door and I had to hold Bev tighter. She took a beating in this house and almost lost her life so the pain was all rushing to her.

"We need to go to your bedroom," Jr. said.

We walked up the stairs and towards the bedroom. There was still crime scene tape on the door. Jr pulled it down and walked inside. We stepped over the blood stain and stood by the window. Jr. lifted the bed and pulled out something strange from the bottom of the box spring.

"What the fuck is that?" I asked.

"It's a fingernail," Jr said holding it up.

"What the fuck was a fingernail doing in my bedroom. Fuzz had some bitch in my room!" Bev snapped.

"Bev calm down. Look at the nail," I said dropping it in her hand.

She looked at it for a few minutes and then I saw the smoke coming out her ears.

"Fuzz didn't kill himself. He was murdered," Jr. said.

"By that bitch Sandra. But how did she get in my house?" Bev asked.

"That is her specialty, she is great at burglaries. How do you think that bitch brought her drugs in the beginning?" I added.

"That bitch killed my husband!" Bev shouted.

"Calm down, we will get them both. They have to go home to get their stash. I will be waiting for them both," Jr. said.

"We need to clean their asses out. Mom told me she was moving money when you went to the hospital," I said.

"I know where they were moving it to. I have been watching them since Jodi told me about Brown. They have been busy. They have about 50 mil in stashes of drugs and money. They were leaving for Mexico on a flight before Puncho was knocked by y'all." Jr. stated.

"How long have you been watching them?" Bev asked.

"D told Jodi about her concerns about a year ago and Jodi called me. I have been on them both since then," Jr. said.

"Damn D, you had my back from the inside," Bev smiled.

"Listen, you're my sister and I will always have your back, even when you don't listen to me," I smiled at her.

"Thank you, can we get out of here?" Bev said.

We walked out, and Jr. dropped us off at the safe house. He was on his way to sit on their new place that we knew nothing about. I gave Jr. the address of the place that only Bev and I knew about. Jr. moved all their shit to a place only the three of us knew about. We learned not to trust anyone after Marquis. Not even G knew about this place.

When we walked in, mom was holding Aaron trying to get him to sleep. He still had a little bruise on his face.

"Well I guess we will both have to explain to our kids that their fathers are dead," she laughed, picking up Aaron from my mom.

"I already told Jr. tonight. He asked so I told him we sent his dad home to see God." She said.

"You miss him, don't you?"

"Of course, I do. He took my virginity. He was my first. But I would kill him all over again and again for his betrayal," I stated.

"Scared of you sis. I don't know what I am going to do," Bev said crying.

"Sis you will get over this in time. What happened?" I asked.

"Fuzz and I met when I got arrested as a teen. And I never cheated on him. He cheated on me several times. And I wait until he is totally committed to me to cheat on him," I cried.

"Listen we never get over that infidelity. But I am not on your side with the G thing. You crossed the line with that one. I understand the need to make him feel the hurt of his cheating and then lying about being paralyzed, but you never choose a best friend. They have been friends since kids," I lectured.

"You're right. I was really wrong. G treated me like a Queen, something that Fuzz never treated me like. I was his ride or die, but never his Queen. I don't know when I fell in love with G, but I did. He always came to the house with flowers for me. Always remembered my birthday. He even spent $50,000 on Aaron. How could I not fall in love with him?" I asked.

"Let me ask you, is Aaron his?"

"Naw, he is Fuzz's. I didn't start flirting with G until after Fuzz was shot. It was at the funeral. Fuzz basically ignored me. G held my hand during the whole service. After that day, I got tired of being treated like just someone that has your last name. And then I got a call from some female and found out that he lied to me about him being paralyzed. I was hurt, hurt beyond repair. The night Fuzz caught us, was the third time we had been together. And I actually broke it off that night. But he snapped. But I don't blame him. I was out of line," Bev cried.

"Listen, no need to cry over spilled milk. But I have to be honest and I don't think that being with G is going to be a good idea," I said.

"I want to break it off, but he won't hear it."

"Well that is too bad, because you can't with him. It sets a bad light on the everything that happened. And how would Aaron look at it later in life?" I asked her seriously.

"I hear you sis. I am going to break it off."

I go up and made us a place as mom washed the kids and put them to bed. Mom had decided to give up her house and move in with us. We needed her now more than ever and I knew that she would be there. But first we really needed to move out of NY. This was no longer the place for us. I figured it might be time for us to move back to Florida. Jr. could handle NY and we could set up shop in Florida. I haven't been out of jail for a week and I was already back in the game, already thinking about my next move. I knew that this life was born into me. What the hell was I thinking about leaving? Now you have both Female Don Dadas in this game. We were about to wreak havoc. I climbed into bed with my mom and Jr. and drifted off to sleep.

Will the Deceit Ever Stop

The next morning, I awoke to my phone going off. Jr., my mother, and the other kids were gone.

"Hello?" I said.

"D, you would not believe what I am looking at right now. I didn't like the way that that pussy boy G was looking at me. So, I followed him." Jr. said into the phone.

"Where are you?" I asked.

"At the place where Puncho and Sandra hide their stash."

"What the fuck is he doing there? I am on my way. If he leaves, follow his ass," I said thinking more betrayal was in the midst.

We go into the car and headed to the spot. Bev was fuming because her husband was dead because of her affair and now G was looking like someone that had something to do with it. I guess she was looking like a fool and feeling that way also. I remember that feeling. I felt that way for a year after Marquis was gone. When we arrived, Jr. was still there. We got out and got into his car.

"He is still in there. I don't know what he is doing. But now that he has seen my face, I didn't want to spook him. I am just watching," Jr. said, pointing to the house.

"I wonder what he is doing in there. I am getting pissed the fuck off right now. This bitch is here, and my husband is dead. If I find out he had something to do with it. I swear he will beg for death!" Bev said with death in her eyes and venom in her voice.

"Well, there is only one way to find out. Let's go!" I said.

Jr. handed us some guns, we checked the clips, and loaded one in the chamber. We all got out and fanned out, surrounding the house. I walked to the window in the front and looked through it. I didn't see any movement, so I slid the window up and slowly crept through it. I looked at the back once my feet hit the floor, and Bev and Jr. was coming in at the same time. We met in the middle of the ranch style house. We didn't hear any noise and wondered where he could be. We looked around carefully and found a set of stairs that lead downstairs. Bev slowly opened the door and peeked down the stairs. We still didn't hear anything. We slowly descended the stairs and peeked around the corner. We still heard nothing. We noticed that there were three doors leading down a dark hallway. Still not hearing anything. We crept to the first door, I slowly opened it, and in the room was a safe. I guess that is where the stash is. There were cameras and surveillance equipment set up in the room. I guess someone was supposed to be watching it or that it recorded. I pulled the plug and closed the door. Jr. opened the next door as we trained our guns on it. There was nothing in the room but a bed and some clothes hanging in the room. I guessed this was where their security person was staying. But, where were they? Bev made her way down to the last door and as she got closer, she heard deep moans. She looked back at us as we steadied our guns. She slowly pulled the door open and I thought that she was about to hit the floor. I grabbed her and looked at what she was looking at. I could barely believe my eyes.

"Well, well, well! What do we have here?" I laughed as Jr. came through the door.

"D, Bev, Jr…look…I…was…just…," G stuttered trying to get the words out.

"I slept with your nasty ass. And I find you bent over a table, with dude fucking the shit out of you! What the fuck??!!!" Bev screamed.

"Bev, what kind of crew did you throw together?" I said laughing.

"I guess a bunch of batty boys!"

"Damn, y'all really know how to pick a crew. A bunch of Homo-thugs!" Jr. laughed.

"Listen Bev..it's really not what you think…I don't do this on a regular..," He lied again stuttering.

"Why, you lying bitch! We been married for years. And what the hell, you fucking some female?" his partner said, rolling his neck.

"Listen, we are not here for you, so you can leave. But he can't," I said.

"You can have him. And you can have the code to his safe also. I don't do the pitching for the other team," his husband said.

"Wait what do you mean, his safe?" Drama asked.

"Puncho and Sandra work for his ass. You don't know about him. This is Sweets," he spilled all the tea.

"What the fuck, you the one that's been after me! I wonder how my mother didn't know who you were," Bev stated.

"That's the power of plastic surgery, you dumb bitch!" he spewed.

That is when Bev lost it. She began to beat his ass unmercifully. I knew that my sister could fight, but not like that. She beat him within an inch of his life, before we stopped her. She tied him up and I took the husband into the other room where he opened the safe, put on his clothes, and left for good. I wasn't too worried about him. After the display of what Bev did to G/ Sweets/whatever his name is, we knew he would never talk.

"Bev, what do you want to do with him now?" I asked holding her while she cried.

"Leave me here. We have unfinished business," she said through clenched teeth.

"I can't do that. What if someone else comes?" I worried.

"I will stay with her and watch the house while she does her business. Drama, you go home to the kids. I will bring her home later. I got her!" Jr. said.

"Ok, I am leaving. Bev, sis, I love you. I will see you at home later." I said kissing her on her tear stained cheek.

I left and went home, worried about Bev's mental health. Her mom was at the house when I got there. We spoke about the whole situation. She filled me into the story.

"I met Sweets after Jr. broke my heart. We were supposed to meet on one of his trips to the states, but he cancelled on me. And I found out it was because he was married and you both were with him. I had planned to tell him that I was pregnant with Bev. You were 2 at the time and so beautiful. And so was your mom. I knew that I couldn't compete with you both. So, I disappeared. Soon after, I met Sweets. We didn't get involved until after Bev was born. He said that he would never date a woman with another man's seed inside. So, we waited. Soon after Bev was born, I got hooked on drugs. He left me, and I slipped into depression. I ran into your mom after your dad died and she basically helped to take care of us. She knew Bev was Jr.'s just by looking at her. The money that the constable sent from Jamaica on a monthly basis, she sent me. She helped me get off drugs and we both made a plan to one day bring you girls together. We both wanted to wait until after we felt that you could handle it. But Fuzz felt that it would be best if he sent her to protect you. Bev is more like your dad. She is cold-hearted. I am shocked that she didn't kill Fuzz. And I am even more shocked that she has a child. I guess you bring out the soft side in her," She said holding my hand.

"We bring out the best in each other. I just wish that we were able to grow up together. Maybe we wouldn't have been in this position now." I added.

"No, it was for the best. Bev was very hot headed, she needed to learn patience. And her going to jail, taught her that. If you would have grown up with her, you would have been just the same. We needed to keep you separated. Jr. had both of you wrapped up inside of him, but he was smart. He was a thinker like you, very caring, and very loving. But he was also cold-hearted and calculating like Bev. Bev is learning how to be more like you, and you are learning to be more like her. We brought you together at the right time." Her mom said.

"Where is Bev now?" My mom asked.

"I left her with Jr. She found out that Sweets was G. So, they have some unfinished business to take care of," I said.

"Wait, what did you say!?" Her mom asked.

"Yes, G turned out to be Sweets. He changed his face and got into her camp. Fuzz and him have been friends for years," I added.

"Wait, now it makes sense. I always wondered why G never wanted to be near me. And I never knew Fuzz and Sweets were the same age," Bev's mom said.

"Fuzz is three years younger that both of you. And so is G, I mean Sweets." I added.

"Now it all makes sense. I always wondered why he called me when she was sixteen. I should have told her about him. I should have told her how he was a part of your dad's death. I messed up. I messed up royally." She began to cry.

"Listen, we can't cry over spilled milk. Bev is taking care of it right now. The past is the past. All that matters now is the future and family. We have decided to leave NY. We are turning it over to Jr. and we want to move to Florida. I want to start over and have the kids soaking up vitamin D all day long. Also, we need a new market," I stated.

"You know I think that is such a great idea. Plus, most of your dad's contacts are still there. I know a few were looking to get out, the last time I was there. Maybe you can take over. Plus, you are closer to Jamaica. It's time you go back and take your rightful place." My mom agreed.

"No, Bev and I can take our rightful place," I stated.

Back at The House

"So, you're the one that got my mom hooked on drugs and had something to do with my dad dying? And I slept with you after you slept with my mom. You're a nasty ass buzzard. But it doesn't matter anymore. Because all of the crew will soon be dead." I smirked.

"Who is the nasty, stupid ass bitch?! You slept with your man's best friend, a faggot, and caused his death. Oh, wait and I slept with your mama," he laughed.

"Yes, you did all of that. And guess what, this stupid bitch is going to be the last person you see," I laughed even harder.

Picking up a bottle of acid that Jr. retrieved from the car and a blow torch, I spent the rest of the night dropping acid on him and lighting it on fire. I promised him the slowest, most painful death that he could wish for before his heart gave out. He pleaded with me to kill him quickly. I fell and cried like a baby. Jr. held me and promised that I would be ok because I had an empire to build. He was right, I was never built like a whiney girl. I was a Pitbull in a skirt since birth. Jr.'s cold-hearted blood ran through my veins and it was time to get his turf back in Jamaica. It was time for me to grab my sister and take over our home.

We got back to the house and all of my weeping was done. I picked up my son and headed to D's room. We needed to talk. It was time for us to take our rightful place on our daddy's throne.

Breaking News out of Jamaica

"Good evening everyone this is Jasmine Campbell reporting live from the street right down from Parliament. We don't know what is going on, but every member of Parliament and the Police department has been beheaded and thrown into the Ocean. Only one member of the Police department was left alive. No one knows who has done this and why. The head Constable is unable to speak at this time. But England has sent some people over to investigate what has happened here. We can't get close enough to see what is going on because as you see the road has been blocked off. We were told that everyone was killed at the same time in their homes. This was a well-organized hit. I will continue to keep you updated as more information comes in.

Pembroke Pines Florida

"Hello?" I asked into the phone.

"Hey, it's done!" Jr. said on the other side of the line.

"Thanks, we will be there in a few days," I said and hung up.

We left one of the constables alive because he was the son of my father's friend. The man that got us out of Jamaica that fateful night. He was part of the plan and next in line to become the next Governor-General. He was already the head of the Army. So, we would throw money to get him elected. We made sure that he shot and killed a pawn to make it look like he was being ambushed but was able to strike first. Everything was working according to plan. We had already brought up most of Barbican and began to set up our operation in Saint Ann's. Our family was happy to have us coming home and was willing to back us. I was even able to buy back our old house. Dennis' family was set up in our house.

"Bev, wake up, it's time to put our plan into motion," I said shaking her.

"Time to go home sis!" She said stretching.

We had lived in Pembroke Pines for nearly two years as we devised our plan to reclaim Jamaica. Two trips and everyone knew that we were Jr.'s girls. We wore his face and his disposition so earning respect was easy. Our reputation in Florida and NY helped us a lot. One look in Bev's eyes and you knew that she had his attitude, and one look in mine showed that I had my sister's back.

We packed for our trip and headed out to Jamaica, while our parents took care of the kids. We decided to all stay together in a ten-acre compound. We owned most of the police departments in southern

Florida and a few up north. Now it was time to spread out more. Going home was bittersweet, but it was time.

We stepped off the plane and were treated like Queens. We changed the Island drastically. Jamaica had never seen so much money flowing into it. There was no more poverty and every child went to school. We built up Jam-one and we knew that dad was smiling on us. Bev even found herself a husband. As for me, I wasn't ready for love just yet. I went back to money being my boyfriend and I found solace in raising and taking care of children.

A Chance meeting

One day I was strolling along the beach in Miami just taking in the fresh cool breeze when I heard a voice behind me.

"Well hello, stranger. Haven't seen you in a while."

"OMG! How have you been? How is the family?" I asked.

"Everyone is fine. But you would know that if you came around more often."

"You are so right. I have been horrible. How is your cousin. I need to call Selena. I haven't seen her in ten years," I said.

"Selena is great, she is married and has 3 kids. She is actually in Miami now. Not too far from here. Do you want me to take you there?" he asked.

"Yes, let me go grab my car," I said.

"No need for that. We can walk to her house from here. She lives right there," he said pointing to a huge house in the distance.

"I walk here all the time, and I can't believe that I haven't run into any of you." I said walking towards Selena's house.

"Yeah that is strange. Marisol lives right there next to Selena," he said.

"OMG, Bev will be so excited to hear this."

"Marisol told me about her. I want to meet the woman that saved my sister," he said.

Antonio was so handsome. I always had a crush on him when we were younger, but I had no interest in boys until I met Marquis.

"Let me call Bev and tell her to meet us over here. What's the address?" I asked.

"Bev you wouldn't believe who lives here in Miami." I said.

"Who?"

"Marisol and Selena!" he screamed.

"For real! Where? I'm coming over."

"I'm going to text you the address. I'm almost there. I am walking with Antonio right now to the house."

"I am on my way!" she said, hanging up.

We walked the rest of the way to Selena's house.

"Hey Sel, guess what I picked up on the beach?" he said peeking into the door.

"I hope it's not more shells, them kids got enough," she laughed with her hand on her hip.

"Do I look like a sea shell to you!" I said laughing.

"OMG where the hell have you been!" she yelled grabbing me and hugging me.

"You wouldn't believe me if I told you," I said laughing.

"Well we have plenty of time to catch up. Marisol, guess what Antonio brought home!" She yelled.

"I hope not more sea shells." Marisol said rounding the corner.

"If ya'll don't stop calling me sea shells!" I laughed.

"Where the hell have you been?" Marisol said hugging me.

"Well when Bev gets here we can discuss everything," I said.

Selena dragged me into the living room just as the doorbell rang. For the next hour, we caught up and told them all about the last five years of activities. Antonio and I took a long walk on the beach as Bev stayed behind. The kids moved with our parents to Jamaica, so we had all night to catch up. Bev's husband came over and we had a ball. That night ended with a kiss between Antonio and I and plans to see each other more.

Two Years later

"Baby, I can see the head. Just one more push!" Antonio screamed at me.

"It's a girl!" The doctor announced.

"She is so beautiful," I said looking at my daughter lying on my chest.

Antonio and I grew closer over the last couple of years and eventually got married. I never thought that I would ever find or want love again. But God has a mysterious way of telling you what he has in store for you. And as you can see, I now have a beautiful baby girl. Business is great, and we finally found our happiness.

20 Years Later

"Ma, I think that it is time for you to retire for good. I am sick of you looking over my shoulder. I got this," Jr. said.

"Jr., I am not looking over your shoulder. I just think that you are moving too fast. You are drawing attention to yourself. You saw what happened to Aaron. God Bless his soul. I lost him and Bev, I don't want to lose you also," I said rubbing his cheek.

"Ma, I know the pain that you feel over losing them. But you have to trust me. With Sole watching over me. We will be fine."

"I never wanted this life for you and your sister. I didn't want to bring you in. Now that Bev and Aaron are gone, I am scared. I am getting old. And all of you are involved. I don't like this," I reiterated.

"Mom, listen. We have all learned from the betrayal that has lived in your heart. We also know that you had to do what you had to do to survive. We also accept it. We all have grandpa's blood in us. You can't stop this. I am not dumb. I have researched this. We got this, trust me!" Jr. said.

I sat at the table and looked at my son and daughter, and Murda's children. This is my family. He was right. They have the blood lines of warriors. It was time for me to let it go. Time for me to retire and enjoy my time with my husband. Bev worked herself to death. After Aaron was shot and killed, she worked overtime not wanting any help finding his killer. Finding him cost both of their lives. Her husband was a mess for nearly a year. He eventually died of a broken heart. I ended up raising their daughter Sharee. I looked at her, and at Sole. They both carried Bev's ruthlessness. They were the assassins, the guns of this family. I have never seen anyone shoot with such precision before. And let's not talk about their hand to hand combat skills. Jr. and Malik had all the knowledge to make and move drugs. And Susan, she had the financial skills and made sure money was always good. I knew they would be fine.

"Ok I am leaving. But I will be close for any advice," I relented.

"Thank you, Ma. We will be fine." Jr. said, hugging me.

Last Breath

The day I took my last breath was the best day of my life. My kids owned the drug game. They took over every country but the Asian ones. I was so proud of them. They did it as a family. Nothing more, nothing less. I died peacefully surrounded by my kids and grandkids on my island, Oasis of Turks and Cacaos where I lived with my husband and grands until he passed away 2 years ago. Antonio filled my days with love and happiness. I was ready to go see him again and enjoy my forever happiness next to him.

Yes, I lived the life that most people want. And I lasted this long because of brains. I left my pride and flashiness at the door and moved in silence. Now my kids move in that same silence. Don't cry for me. I have lived longer and fuller than most in this game. I am and always will be the Female Don Dada......